Blood of Lions

A Garrett Storm Novel

C. Marten-Zerf

Anglo American Press

LONDON, UNITED KINGDOM

Anglo American Press
London
England
United Kingdom

Book Layout © 2017 BookDesignTemplates.com

Blood of Lions/ C. Marten-Zerf/Craig Zerf. -- 1st ed.
ISBN 978-0-0000000-0-0

Once again –

For my wife, Polly and my

son, Axel

Your light chases the

shadows from my soul.

Romans 13:4 - *For he is the minister of God to thee for good. But if thou do that which is evil, be afraid; for he beareth not the sword in vain: for he is the minister of God, a revenger to execute wrath upon him that doeth evil.*

This is a novel…that means I made it up, however…many of the people mentioned do actually exist. You all know who you are. Some of the scenes and places have been deliberately changed, this was done for two reasons, firstly to protect the identity of some involved and secondly as a narrative tool. If you would like to discuss the reality then please drop me an email at zuffs@sky.com

There was a festival atmosphere about the procession. Five Toyota pickup trucks each towing a converted horse trailer. The first four trailers each contained approximately two and a half tons of Southern White Rhinoceros. *Ceratotherium simum simum.* The largest living land mammal after the African Elephant. Five thousand pounds of pissed-off-Pachyderm reduced to the state of a docile pet dog by the introduction of 2 milligrams of Acepromazine, via a dart gun.

The fifth trailer had two occupants. The game rangers had already dubbed them Dick and Dom. A pair of male rhino calves. Overlarge three toed feet, massive upright ears and tiny little nubs of horn. They too were sedated and lay snuggled together, snoring and whistling in their sleep, their juvenile lips turned up into permanent half-smiles as they gamboled and capered in their dreams.

The rangers had round up the Rhinos that morning, tracking them through the night and darting them as soon as the sun had risen to provide enough light to shoot by.

And now they were on their way to the Kharma Rhino reserve in Botswana. It had been deemed of vital importance to move as many rhino to Kharma as possible. This was due to the fact that well over one thousand Rhino had been killed in South Africa the year before, whereas there had not been one death in the Kharma Rhino Reserve in the entire twenty-four years since its inception.

Unfortunately, due to the vast amounts of red tape, combined with the lack of both funds and manpower, the parks trust had only managed to relocate a mere six rhino during the last twelve months. A failure to perform that bordered on the ridiculous.

Malusi was riding shotgun in the second pick up; his Remington pump action lay across his knees. Since his recent qualification from the South African Wildlife College and his being hired as a conservation officer by the Kruger National Game Park, this was the most exciting day that he had ever experienced.

He was convinced that the future of the country that he loved would come to rely more and more on the tourist industry and as far as he could see, the tourist industry in Africa would be dominated by tourists seeking the wild game experience.

That, combined with his genuine love of animals, is what had driven him to study and to pursue his current career.

The convoy drove slowly and carefully down the rutted dirt roads that led from the reserve. The morning sun blasted the land with a white-hot heat that robbed the scenery of all shadow, rendering the vista as a flat, two-dimensional photograph, printed in shades of browns and olive-greens and khakis.

The dust from the lead pickup hung in the dead air like a massive ochre storm cloud, coating all the followers in its fine, yellow-brown talc.

Malusi placed the butt of the Remington on the floor between his legs and pointed the barrel out of the window. Each pick up had a driver and a passenger that had been issued with a weapon. Malusi had his shotgun, and the remaining rangers carried the venerable R1 assault rifle. A weapon that had last seen service in the 1980's during the South African bush war.

They all handled their weapons with a certain amount of familiarity, but it was patently obvious that they were not professional soldiers. A few hours on the range does not a military man make. These were Game Rangers. People trained in conservation and animal husbandry. Weapons were there for defense against wild animals and even then, only as a very final resort.

But, as rhino poaching had become so endemic, the rangers had been forced to swap their 375 bolt action hunting rifles and shotguns for weapons more suited to warfare than to animal control.

Malusi glanced upwards, squinting through the dust-covered windscreen. High above them wheeled a White Backed Vulture, a magnificent bird with a wingspan of over seven feet. It had been following them since they had set off that morning.

The young Zulu shivered with superstitious dread. The vulture was never a good omen. Particularly one showing such persistence.

The land mine was a Chinese version of the type 72. Twelve pounds of high explosive jammed into a steel container. It was capable of damaging a main battle tank to the point of putting it out of service.

Its effect on the thin-skinned Toyota commercial vehicle was nothing short of catastrophic.

The blast severed the cab from the load area, tossing it up into the air in a storm of steel and flame. Both the driver and passenger were killed instantly as the shock wave smashed their brains, shattered their bones and crushed their internal organs. The trailer and rhino that they were pulling crashed into the back half of the vehicle and flipped over, landing on its side. Even though the rhino was sedated it screamed and bellowed in terror, thrashing its massive head from side to side, slashing its flesh open on the jagged exposed blades of metal sticking out of the sides of the damaged trailer.

The gigantic shock wave punched Malusi's driver in the chest, causing him to spasm at the wheel, jerking the pickup into a hard right-hand skid. The trailer jack-knifed behind them, tearing itself off the hitch and rolling into their vehicle.

Malusi kicked the door open, stepped outside and stood, swaying, next to the ruined cab. His mouth hung open as his brain tried desperately to catch up with the surrounding reality.

The other pick-ups came to a halt and men started to jump out and run towards him. He saw their mouths working and he knew that they were talking to him. Shouting even. But his ears were ringing and the huge amounts of sensory overload had caused auditory exclusion and tunnel vision.

He shook his head and, all of a sudden, sound and vision returned.

And then the air around them came alive with the spiteful crack and buzz of high velocity metal. Bright scars appeared in the door of the pick up and one of the other game rangers flew backwards as his body was riddled with shot, blood spraying from him in a viscous mist of bright red.

Someone shouted. 'Machine gun.'

Malusi grabbed his shotgun from the cab and looked for someone to shoot at but, before he could, his breath was driven from his body as three copper-jacketed steel rounds slammed into him, picking him up and throwing him over the hood of the vehicle.

Some of the rangers began to return fire but they were soon cut down by the overwhelming quantity of ordinance arrayed against them.

Malusi slid down off the hood and lay on the dry African earth. An ant crawled over his open eye. He tried to blink but he couldn't. He wondered if he was breathing. And if so, how? He could hear his heart beating. A drawn-out rushing sound. Like water being drawn from a hand-pump. Slow and laborious.

He could hear men talking. Laughing. He smelled cigarettes.

Then the sound of a petrol driven chain saw starting up. The ragged growl of machinery.

The horrific sound of the saw hacking through flesh and bone. The bellowing of the rhinos. A volley of shots.

'The horns,' whispered Malusi to himself. 'They're cutting out the horns.'

He tried to move.

He had to do something.

He had to stop this.

A shadow fell over him. Someone was standing there.

'Hey, check this out,' they said.

A strange accent. Russian? Polish?

'This fucker's still alive.'

'Kill him.'

'No,' whispered Malusi. 'Please.'

He felt a boot against his face. A push. Rolling him over onto his back. The barrel of a rifle. Held close to his eye. So close as to be out of focus.

You never hear the sound of the shot that kills you.

***

The vulture was patient.

It sat in the thorn tree and waited.

Eventually the men left and quiet settled once more over the African veld. It flapped its large wings as it dropped to the ground.

Spoiled for choice it simply waddled over to the nearest body and started to feed.

Malusi had been right - the bird had been a bad omen.

The worst.

Tai Zeng stood still and waited for his attackers to come to him. There were three of them. Large men. Each one topping his mere five foot five by more than six inches.

The first one struck out. A straight punch to Tai's head. A powerful blow that would knock the smaller man to ground. Once down it would be easy to dispatch him with either a stamping kick or a simple snap kick to his head.

But the punch never landed.

Tai moved inside the swing and, using the tips of his fingers, he delivered a *Fut Sao* blow to his opponent's underarm. Striking where the lymph nodes, arteries and veins conglomerated. The man stiffened and fell to the floor as his entire nervous system simply shut down. Tai casually kicked him in the side of the head as he stepped over him, making sure that he was completely out of the fight.

Again, Tai stood still, the only part of him moving were his eyes as they flicked between his two remaining opponents.

They both attacked at once, driving in from opposite sides, hoping to confuse the master.

But it was to no avail. Tai launched a counter attack, smashing his open hand into the one man's Brachial Plexus on the side of his neck. Cutting off his blood supply and incapacitating him with a single blow.

Then he swivelled and, using the Ving Tsun Kung Fu method of rolling punches, he drove the final opponent backwards, throwing five punches in under a second. It was like being hit by a machine gun and the man was unconscious before his limp body even reached the floor.

Tai Zeng stared down at the three unconscious victims, his face a mask of scorn. The three men had been personally recommended by the local dojo as sparring partners worthy of respect. They were far from it. Rank amateurs.

Tai had studied *Ving Tsun* under the auspices of the late master Ip Man. It was an explosive fighting style that combined close quarter combat with solid defensive techniques and rapid counter strikes. It had been popularised during the late seventies by the film star Bruce Lee and many westerners referred to it as Wing Chun Kung Fu or often simply, Kung Fu.

Typically, the western mind had, once again, misunderstood the entire concept. Kung Fu referred to any skill that takes time to master. Only westerners thought of Kung Fu as unique to the martial arts.

Tai grabbed a small hand towel and left the dojo, wiping the sweat from his face as he did so. He closed the door behind him and walked to his desk, throwing the towel to the floor.

Pressing the button to his intercom he buzzed his secretary.

'Mingyu. Come through.'

While he waited, he stood at the floor to ceiling window and gazed at the view. One hundred stories below him, Victoria Harbor stretched from left to right, crowded with all manner of boats from ancient Junks to modern Sunseekers. It was a vibrant mélange of both color and culture.

The skyline was dominated by the massive brooding hulk of Mount Austin, or The Peak as it was known locally.

But the view had little to do with why Tai leased the ultra-expensive office space on the 100th floor of the International Commerce Centre in Kowloon. He was there for other reasons. It was the tallest building in Hong Kong and it shared its address with prestigious firms like Morgan Stanley and Credit Suisse. Highly respected international companies that Tai Zeng felt himself to be on a par with.

The floors 102 - 118 were leased by the 5-star Hong Kong Ritz Carlton hotel in which Tai leased a permanent three bedroom suite at a cost of five thousand dollars a night. Although that was his permanent residence, he also had a one hundred- and twenty-foot

Sunseeker yacht berthed at The Royal Hong Kong Yacht Club, one of the city's most exclusive clubs. Yet another accoutrement that he had acquired more because he thought that it was the correct thing to do, rather than any love for the water, or for seagoing dwellings.

Mingyu entered through the main office door and closed it behind her. Barely topping four feet in height, she was like a person in miniature. A neat boyish figure and short black bob. She wore no makeup save for a thick line of kohl around her large brown eyes. Her lightweight cotton dress reached just below her knees, loose fitting and plain. No jewellery.

'Mingyu. I need you to book me a flight to Vietnam. Next week. Two-day stay. Same hotel as always. Also, set up a meeting with the Police Commissioner as soon as. Mutual ground. Perhaps one of the restaurants in the hotel. I need to speak to colonel Chang sometime this afternoon, check out the time difference between here and Zimbabwe and place the call around four o'clock our time.

Tai droned on, dictating a long list of tasks for his tiny assistant. She took no notes but simply nodded at the end of each command to show that she had taken it in.

While Tai talked, he slowly stripped off. Peeling his sweat-wet training clothes from his body until he was completely naked. Then he grabbed the diminutive Mingyu, bent her over the desk and pulled her dress up around her waist. She wore no underwear. He entered her roughly, grunting with the effort as he continued to dictate his seemingly endless list of tasks.

Mingyu didn't react at all, save to keep nodding at the appropriate times.

When he was finished, he withdrew, wiped himself off with his discarded shirt and waved a dismissal to Mingyu.

She bowed once and left the room, her dark eyes expressionless. Her face a mask of blank submissiveness. All feelings buried deep by the large monthly check that she received combined with the knowledge that people did not resign from the employ of Tai Zeng. You worked for him until he retired you.

And one did not want to be retired by mister Zeng.

Tai crossed the office to his built-in closet and selected a traditional black silk Zhongshan Zhuang or Chinese Tunic Suit, as favoured by Chairman Mao. He slipped his feet into a pair of silk slippers and then poured himself a drink. Two fingers of the ubiquitous Johnnie Walker King George V that was so popular amongst the Hong Kong elite. No ice.

He sat at his desk and savoured the smoky taste. It hadn't been so long ago when his entire month's earnings didn't come close to being enough to afford a single bottle of the premium spirits. Growing up in Kwun Tong along with over half a million other dispossessed people, crammed into an area hardly capable of supporting even a tenth of that number.

He remembered well those first days in the gangs. Barely a teenager, he had been accepted as a Blue Lantern in the local Triads. An uninitiated member, lowest of the low. Called on to do all of the worst jobs. But he worked hard and soon became known as a youngster to rely on. An up-and-coming member who never refused a task no matter how dangerous or humiliating.

He had been promoted to the level of a 49'er before anyone else that had joined with him and as an initiated Triad member, was exposed to his first tastes of both power and privilege.

Within a few short years he achieved the rank of Enforcer, a rank on a par with a White Paper Fan administrator or a Straw Sandal liaison officer. It was at this stage that Tai decided to branch out on his own. The Triad system, unlike the Italian Cosa Nostra, is more than happy for its members to go their own way, as long as they retain a loose affiliation to the Triad structure and pay their dues every month.

Now Tai ran his own empire. Even though his rank in the Triads had never officially been raised, he was considered by all to be at least on a level with a Vanguard or Operations officer and perhaps even as high as the Deputy Mountain Master, who was second in charge.

Tai's main strength was his innate ability to plan for the future. He played the long game in a structure that so often looked for the quick profit. The big score. As such he had used his growing influence to inveigle his way into the new Red Chinese government structure that now controlled Hong Kong, sowing his seeds and laying his lines of influence and power in all aspects from customs and excise, to police and military envoys.

As a result, when China had started their big military push into Africa; Tai Zeng had been there, riding on the coat tails of the People's Army.

Now he owned, to all intents and purposes, his own crack military team whom he used to control his substantial interests in the region.

Officially the team were actually a part of the People's Army and were ostensibly under the control of Colonel Jin Chang.

Colonel Chang had been transferred to Zimbabwe along with his assistant, Master Sergeant Lu Feng and a detachment of thirty-two Nanjing Flying Tiger special forces troops as a roving fast reaction squad to provide security and advice to the Zimbabwean army.

In reality colonel Chang and his detachment were simply another cog in the mechanism that made up Tai Zeng's criminal engine. And Tai ensured Chang's loyalty by paying him vast amounts of money and allowing him to pursue his own private business ventures as well.

Although Tai had his fingers in many pies including illicit diamond buying, drugs, ivory and prostitution, his main income was generated through the illegal poaching and distribution of Rhino horn.

He had teamed up with a Ukrainian gangster by the name of Viktor Hubenko and together, they were responsible for the deaths of around ten rhinos a week. At the going price of one hundred and twenty thousand dollars per horn, this equated to six million dollars a month, or seventy-two million a year. This, combined with his other criminal pursuits grossed over one hundred million dollars per anum.

But the money was not that important to Tai. Even though he lived a relatively lavish lifestyle he found it hard, if not impossible, to spend more than ten million a year. The rest of his income was a mere set of numbers on a scorecard. A handicap level at golf, a social ranking.

A way to distance himself from the poor shoeless orphan brought up in the slums of Kwun Tong.

Garrett had been the game warden on the laird's estate for over five years now. He had known the laird for most of his life and he owed him more than he could ever repay. He had taken Garrett in when his parents died, leaving him an orphan at the age of ten. The laird sent Garrett to the same boarding school his sons had attended, and he had supported Garrett's decision to join the British army.

There had been a long period, a few years, when he had lost touch with the young soldier. It was during this time, when Garrett had had retired from the army and had pursued far more lucrative work as a private con-tractor, or mercenary soldier, fighting mainly in Africa, a continent that was rife with constant conflict.

The lifestyle had not been good to Garrett, driving him deep into the black heart of war, stripping him to the bone and exposing his dark inner core. Unleashing a violence that ran fast and furious through his soul. Releasing a Beast that found itself capable of the most violent of deeds and actions.

Finally, Garrett had escaped from Africa. Running from his own lack of humanity. Hiding from The Beast.

The laird had taken him in, given him a job as his gamekeeper. He had sensed that Garrett needed help but he had never questioned him. Never pushed him. He had simply allowed him free rein.

Garrett soon discovered that The Beast was an integral part of himself and you cannot run from yourself. So, he locked it up in a cage and refused to feed it. And he lived alone. Not lonely but singularly, at one with the Highlands. The outdoors.

However, there were still times when The Beast crashed through the bars and came out into the light.

Bad times.

Garrett tried to avoid them.

But sometimes they were thrust upon him.

That morning his laird had come to him. His granddaughter had gone missing. She had been incommunicado for almost a month now. There was no huge panic on. It was suspected that she was with her boyfriend, a ne'er-do-well that she had met after she had dropped out of university. A small-time drug dealer, and even smaller time artist, some twelve years her senior.

Garrett had never met him, but he knew Alicia well. A product of the most expensive private schools combined with almost unlimited access to wealth. Her parents would describe her, if they bothered, as willful, fiery and possessed of her own mind.

Garrett, on the other hand, would describe her as a stone cold, spoiled brat.

The laird doted on her and, in all fairness, he was the only human being that she treated with anything approaching respect.

Regardless, the laird had asked Garrett to track her down, and there was no way that he would ever refuse him.

He had been provided with Alicia's cell number. He tried it and it had gone straight through to messages. The only other info he had was the last known address of her waster boyfriend, Rafe Hinds.

Now Garrett was currently heading for that current address, in the estate Defender Land Rover. He had been on the road for over three hours, driving through the lashing rain, the skies as gray as the Atlantic Ocean, visibility less than fifty yards and the merest hint of sun, so weak as to necessitate the use of headlamps even during the day.

He was using a satellite navigation system and it informed him that he was nearing his destination. A road in the notorious East End area of Glasgow.

Garrett had never been there before, but he did remember hearing that a man born in that deprived area had a life expectancy some nine years less than a man born in rural India.

The area itself was a depressing mélange of old and new and completely fucked up. Crumbling tenement blocks next to unfinished new builds and dilapidated Victorian houses. He drove past a building that looked derelict but, as he got closer, he saw a hand painted sign, lit up by a red spotlight. The sign said, "Adult Fun".

A monstrous doorman stood outside the rotting wooden front door, rain sluicing off his black mackintosh. Shining his shaven head. Dripping unheeded from his broken nose. He stared as Garrett drove by. Eyes like two pebbles in a mountain of flesh. Gorilla in the mist.

Three hundred yards further on he reached his destination. A row of seedy Victorian houses. Red brick and broken sash windows. Tottering chimneys. Front doors scabbed by peeling paint. Drifts of refuse. Milk cartons, crisp packets, newspapers, used condoms. Needles.

Garrett felt his first niggles of worry. He had known that Alicia had fallen in with a less than salubrious bunch, but he had always understood it to be an upper-class dalliance with the lower middle classes. Nothing too rough or untoward. A childish poke in the eye or middle finger to parents considered too cold or distant or remote.

A callow cry for attention.

But this area and the vista that presented itself to him at the moment smacked of something deeper. People who lived in places like this did not do so through choice or through rebellion. People who lived in a shithole like this did so because they had nowhere else to go.

They had no further to fall.

Garrett pulled up against the sidewalk, stepped out, locked the door behind him and headed to the second house along. Number 223.

The door, at one stage, had been red. Now it was a pale pink. A badly painted anarchy sign had been scrawled across it and, under that, a swastika.

The swastika had been painted incorrectly so that one of the arms went the wrong way.

A billboard to both ignorance and stupidity.

He thought about knocking but then decided against it and simply tried the door. It was open, the lock long since smashed and hanging free. He pushed it and walked in.

The building stank of damp and sweat and urine. And something else. Some sweet undefined stench. Heady yet, at the same time, nauseating. Garrett was not familiar with it.

He walked carefully through the ground floor, opening doors and peering into rooms. Three rooms downstairs, all uninhabited.

There was also a kitchen. An old ceramic sink, cracked, half full of an unidentifiable black oily substance. A few broken cupboards. An old refrigerator. The door open. Bizarrely, the internal fridge light still worked and it shone brightly from inside the white, glossy interior. A pathway to another world.

There was a bathroom. The bath had been removed. If it had been an old cast iron one then it had most probably been sold for scrap. There was also a toilet. Water ran from the top of the cistern, the flow mechanism long since broken and the plumbing continued to attempt to fill an already overfull tank. The toilet itself was blocked with an old T-shirt that had obviously been used when toilet paper had run out. Garrett grimaced at the smell and left the room, heading for the stairs.

He climbed the creaking staircase and started to search the next floor. The first room, like the ones below, was empty.

When he entered the next room, he almost didn't recognize her.

She sat crossed legged on the floor. Her long blonde hair had been hacked short and her eyes were sunken into their sockets. A lava lamp bubbled away in the corner, distorting the shadows and painting all in the hues of a nightmare. Blood red and frozen blue.

The floor was slick with vomit, the stench sweet and rotten at the same time. Garrett had seen this before. It was a fairly common side effect from injecting heroin. But to the user, the minor inconvenience of throwing up all over yourself was inconsequential compared to the resultant high.

There were two other people in the room. Both men. They sat together on a single bed, passing a joint between them.

'Who the fuck are you?' one asked.

Garrett ignored him completely.

'Alicia,' he said. His voice low. Non-threatening. 'Your grandfather is worried about you. He's been trying to call.'

The young girl stared at him for a while. 'Where's he?'

'He's at home,' answered Garrett. 'He asked me to find you. To take you home.'

She shook her head. 'Not going home.'

'I think that you should, Alicia. Just to show him that you're okay. You don't have to stay.'

Again, she shook her head. 'No. Stay here.'

'You heard her,' said one of the men from the bed. 'So, fuck off now, why don't you?'

Once again Garrett merely ignored him. 'Come on, Alicia. You can't stay here. It's not good. Come back with me. Speak to the laird. No worries. Things will be alright.'

The man who had been talking to Garrett stood up off the bed, walked over and grabbed him by the shoulder.

'Look, mate. Fuck off before I make you fuck off.'

Garrett didn't bother to even look at the man. He simply backhanded him across his face. Blood sprayed from the man's smashed nose as the blow lifted him up and deposited him back on the bed. Unconscious.

Alicia screamed. The other man jumped off the bed and ran from the room.

'You hit Rafe,' shouted Alicia.

She jumped up and ran over to the prostrate man, patting ineffectually at his face in an attempt to revive him, tears welling from her eyes.

'He's hurt. You hurt him.'

She attacked Garrett, both hands swinging at him, pummeling him in the chest and shoulders.

Garrett stood and accepted the abuse. Eventually she ran out of energy and slumped down onto the bed.

'Sorry,' said Garrett. 'He'll be fine. Alicia, you need to come back with me.'

'Fuck you.'

Garrett shook his head. 'Afraid not, my girl. Now look, I don't want to get all demanding and asshole about the whole thing, but the laird asked me to get you home, so there is no longer any choice in the matter. You are coming back with me. Accept it, embrace it, argue with your grandfather. I am simply the messenger.'

'You can't tell me what to do,' she hissed at him. 'You're just the hired help. A jumped-up gardener. Fuck you, you servant.'

Garrett nodded. 'That's correct. I am a servant. But I am not your servant, Alicia. I serve your grandfather. So, pack your shit, or don't, we are leaving.'

As Garrett finished speaking the bedroom door crashed open. The runner and four more men walked in. The runner had called in reinforcements. Garrett could see instantly that the four newcomers were a different breed. True bottom feeders. These were not artists experimenting with different levels of consciousness. Nor were they upper-class brats falling off the rails.

These were the real deal. Men who had grown up hard and gotten harder. Tempered through poverty and prison. Through gang wars and institutional violence. Urban hyenas.

And even lions are wary of hyenas.

Garrett stepped back, placing his back into a corner. Cutting down their field of attack.

'Who the fuck do you think you are?' shouted one of the newcomers. Shaven headed, sleeve tattoos. Enough metal in his face to satiate an inner-city scrap merchant. 'You can't come in here and harass my peeps. You made yourself a big mistake.'

Garrett held up his hands. 'Look, mate. I'm sorry. Didn't mean to offend. I've simply come to pick up Alicia. We'll go, no more trouble. Okay?'

The man shook his head. 'No. Not okay. Firstly, you disrespect my peeps, you disrespect me and my boys. And if you disrespect me and my boys then we gotta teach you a lesson.'

As he spoke, he drew a knife from his belt, flicking it open with a well-practiced movement. Behind him his boys also drew their knives.

'Listen, Aaron,' said Alicia. 'He's just a fucking moron. He works for my grandfather. Let him go. He won't come back.'

Aaron looked at Alicia and smiled. 'You're too soft hearted, babe,' he said. 'You don't understand the rules. He dissed us so he gotta pay.'

'Look,' said Garrett. 'There's no need for all of this. Tell you what, you guys back down, I take Alicia and that is that. No one loses.'

'No,' countered Aaron. 'I got a better idea. I cut you real bad, you learn a lesson. You lose.'

Garrett sighed. He had attempted to negotiate. He had done all that he could to offer the hyenas a soft option. But they had refused. Now, all that would happen is they would work themselves up until they were angry enough to do something, and then they would attack. Probably not all at once. In all likelihood, Aaron, who was obviously the leader, would strike first and then the others would barrel in straight afterwards.

Garrett decided to hurry the whole process on and simply stepped forward and punched Aaron.

A straight right, using the power of his hips and shoulders. Striking with the full weight of his hyper-toned, two hundred and twenty pounds of sinew and muscle. Driving a knotted fist of rock-hard calloused bone into Aaron's nose. Crushing it almost completely flat and rendering its owner immediately unconscious for the foreseeable future.

Garrett stepped back from Aaron's prostrate body. Pausing to, once again, give an out to the remaining hyenas. Another offer of the soft option.

It was a mistake.

The sound of the safety catch to a Browning Hi-Power 9mm semi-automatic pistol being released is infinitesimally small. Probably akin to a damp match being broken in half. Or a copper penny being dropped onto a carpet.

But to Garrett it was as loud as a shouted profanity in a church.

He had heard that exact, or similar, sound so many times in his life that it was as common as the sound of a friend's breath. A lover's cough. An undertaker's knock.

It was the sound of imminent death.

Without warning The Beast crashed through the bars of its prison. Howling and slobbering it ran free.

Free to hunt.

Free to fight.

Free to kill.

Garrett grabbed the pistol and yanked it hard sideways, snapping the gunman's finger with a sharp crack. Then he twisted the gun back and away from him with a savage punch, literally tearing the gunman's finger off.

The dismembered finger dropped to the floor and blood arced across the room as the man sank to his knees, squealing in shock and agony. Garrett kept hold of the weapon, grasping it by the barrel.

Then, using the pistol as a club he hammered it into the second man's temple, dropping him to the floor like a felled tree.

The third man received an elbow to the nose and then a savage blow to the top of his head as Garrett clubbed him into unconsciousness.

The runner, true to form, sprinted from the room and ran out into the street as self-preservation wiped all thoughts of heroism from him in one sphincter-tightening moment.

Garrett flipped the pistol over, grabbing it by the butt. Then he stood over the gunman, the barrel pointed unwaveringly between his eyes.

The ex-soldier's expression was bleak. Uncaring. Savage and primeval.

The gunman shook his head. 'No. Please.'

Garrett shook slightly as he fought for ascendancy. Fought for control.

Then, in three swift movements he stripped the pistol, throwing the barrel out of the window and dropping the frame and magazine to the floor.

'Alicia,' he said. His green eyes bored into her, flaying her. Exposing her.

'Yes,' she whispered.

'Let's go.'

She followed him meekly as he led her to the Land Rover, opened her door and strapped her seatbelt on.

He wasn't even breathing hard.

It took them four hours to drive home. During that time neither of them spoke. Garrett because he had nothing that he wanted to say. His job was done. He would take Alicia back to the main house and the laird would take care of things from thereon.

Alicia said nothing because she was already starting to yearn for another fix.

A needle to bring back the sunshine and drive back the oceans of her monstrous self-pity. A balm for her rampant selfishness. A band-aid to plaster over her self-evident stupidity.

Garrett's cell phone rang and he glanced at the incoming number and then picked it up. Eschewing the hands-free in order to have a private conversation that excluded Alicia.

'Petrus, my friend,' he greeted. 'Wassup?'

There was a pause filled only by the familiar echo and boom of the intercontinental satellite link and then the Zulu spoke.

'Hello, *Isosha*,' he said, using Garrett's Zulu nickname, The Soldier. 'I am sorry, but I have bad news. My youngest brother, Malusi. He is dead.'

Even across the thousands of intervening miles Garrett could hear Petrus' pain. The pain of losing a family member. The pain of losing a brother. The pain of losing a friend.

'I am so sorry. How did it happen?'

'He was murdered,' answered Petrus. 'Killed by savages.'

There was silence for a while. Garrett was not sure what to say.

'The body has already been laid out,' continued Petrus. 'The funeral is on Saturday.'

'I will be there,' said Garrett.

'Thank you,' answered Petrus. 'Thank you very much.'

Garrett ended the call and shifted down a gear. Eager to get home.

CHAPTER FOUR

Garrett had hired a car at the airport. A standard, rear wheel drive Ford Focus. He had tried all of the rental outlets but they were all out of four-wheel drives.

So he had hired a small family saloon and resorted to simply thrashing the engine when he got to the rough roads that approached Petrus' village.

When he reached his destination there were already upwards of twenty other vehicles parked there, some four hundred yards from the main kraal. A bevy of small boys stood around the parked cars, preventing other younger children from touching them and also giving directions to any newcomers.

When Garrett stepped out of his car, two of them ran over.

'*Sawabona, baba,*' greeted the one. 'Mister Petrus has been waiting for you. Come with us, please.'

He walked with them, going up the hill to the chief's kraal. They led him through the gate, past the huts that housed the unmarried boys and girls, around the central cattle enclosure and up to one of the larger huts at the far end of the Umuzi.

Malusi's hut was situated four away from the chief's mother's hut, which was, as tradition dictated, the largest of all of the huts. The second largest was the chief's and then the first, second and third wives were housed in abodes of a similar size.

The fact that Malusi's hut was so close to the chief was indicative of his standing as one of the favorite sons, despite his young age.

Petrus' hut was situated near the entrance, next to the watchtower. A small, unpainted residence, big enough to fit two people and Petrus' meager belongings.

However, despite his lack of favor with his father, the chief, Petrus was still both highly respected and well feared. When he spoke, people listened, no matter what their official rank.

And in a nation of warriors, he was still considered paramount.

The Zulu stood up from his vigil outside his brother's hut and walked up to Garrett. Wordlessly they embraced and then Garrett squatted down with Petrus and they sat in silence for a while. Contemplating their own mortality as the mourners filed slowly past the closed hut, showing their respect for the murdered son.

It was the third day and the mourners had been parading past for the last two days now and many thousands had showed their respects.

Before the ceremony had begun, Malusi has been washed and his wounds cleaned and the *Inyanga*, traditional healer, had smeared the black *Insizi* paste on his body and placed some in his right hand to protect him from dark magic.

The *Inyanga* approached the two squatting men. He was leading a full-grown ox. Behind him walked Petrus' father. The chief. As he walked by people, they prostrated themselves full length on the earth and voiced his praises.

'It is time,' said the healer to Petrus.

The ox was led to the entrance to Malusi's hut. It stood, its head held high, its coat glossy with health. A massive beast, worthy of a chief's son.

The *Inyanga* held his arms wide and looked up to the skies.

'Here is the ox,' he intoned. 'The family is cleansing your wounds from the pool of blood in order that you be accepted by your forefathers and ancestors.'

The crowd responded as one.

'*Yebo.*'

Then Petrus stepped forward. His face a stone mask although his eyes glittered with fettered emotion.

'We have come to clean you today from your wounds. With this ox we invite you to join the ancestors and your family. And by the blood of this ox, I swear both revenge and retribution so that your spirit shall be allowed to sit next to your ancestors and be forever at peace.'

Then he took his assegai and, with one firm swipe, dragged it across the ox's throat, severing its carotid artery. The beast fell to its knees and Petrus flipped the assegai over, switching his grip. Then he struck downwards, driving the wide, razor-sharp blade through the thick vertebrae at the top of its neck, killing it instantly.

Without pause, the *Inyanga* and three assistants skinned the animal, rolling it onto a large tarpaulin, working with practiced efficiency.

When they had finished, they took the hide and went into Malusi's hut. The four of them wrapped the murdered son's body in the green hide, binding it tightly and speaking many words of magic over it as they did so.

Meanwhile, another four young men, under the command of the chief's mother, were busy butchering the ox, slicing it into steak-sized pieces and piling it high onto wooden platters.

Almost two tons of steaming, bleeding meat.

Rows of fires had been started and piles of sharpened sticks readied so that the meat could be threaded on and held over the fires to cook.

Two more assistants were generously salting the meat and still more were bringing in countless gallons of traditional beer. Thick, porridge-like maize beer, sour and heady and nutritious.

There were no vegetables and they were not missed. There is no such thing as a Zulu vegetarian, just as there is no such thing as a gun-shy Texan.

The feasting and drinking carried on through the night and well into the next day.

Then, at the sunset of the fourth day, Malusi was brought from his hut and buried in the kraal, a privilege reserved only for the chief and his immediate family.

After the burial, Petrus took a burning brand from one of the fires and set light to Malusi's hut, burning it and its contents to the ground. At the same time, he sliced a lock of hair from his head and cast it into the flames. All of the other members of the family did the same.

Then, as the conflagration turned to embers, family members shaved their heads. This was to show that, although death had occurred, life would continue, just as their hair would grow back.

The chief ordered more meat to be provided. Sheep and goats were slaughtered, the fires were built up and more beer appeared.The drinking and feasting continued unabated for another three days.

On the sunrise of the eighth day, Petrus came to the small hut that Garrett had been provided, knocking respectfully at the entrance as was customary. Garrett, who was already awake, bent down through the low doorway and squatted outside next to his friend.

Petrus also squatted down. He took out a pack of Gauloise cigarettes. Garrett's brand of choice. He opened, extracted two, lit both and passed one to the soldier.

'So,' said Garrett. 'It is over?'

Petrus shook his head. 'No. It has barely begun.'

'Really? What next?'

'My brother cannot rest yet. Even now he wanders the earth, a shade in between life and death. Rejected by the living, unaccepted by the ancestors. And until his death has been avenged, he will remain thus. It is up to me as the oldest brother to seek vengeance. Once that has been achieved then Malusi will sit beside our ancestors.'

'Who will help you?' asked Garrett.

'It is my task alone,' answered Petrus.

'Never,' interjected the soldier. 'I'm not letting you do that alone. I'm with you.'

Petrus smiled. 'It will be dangerous.'

Garrett shrugged. 'Danger is my middle name.'

Petrus raised an eyebrow. 'Really?'

'No,' denied Garrett. 'It's just an expression.'

'Bloody stupid expression,' said Petrus. 'Doesn't make any sense.'

'True,' admitted Garrett. 'So, when do we start?'

'Now,' said Petrus.

Garrett stood up.

CHAPTER FIVE

Colonel Jin Chang and his sergeant, Lu Feng sat in the air-conditioned cab of the XL2060 Fierce Dragon, a Chinese copy of the American Humvee. They were parked on the outskirts of Beit Bridge or Mzingwane as it was called by many of the locals.

Behind the colonel's Fierce Dragon stood two type 63 APC's. In each armored personal carrier sat fifteen Nanjing Flying Tiger Special Forces troops. Two more of the troops sat in the Fierce Dragon with the colonel and the master sergeant, a driver and an assistant.

Chang was waiting for Yarik & Igor to arrive with their latest shipment of rhino horn.

The interior of the vehicle was dense with blue-white smoke. Both Chang and Feng chain smoked. Camel plain, imported from South Africa. If they had been waiting in the same place a couple of decades before, the odds were that they would both have been smoking locally made Rhodesian cigarettes, the to-bacco once heralded as the finest in the world.

But now the tobacco industry was all but defunct, the land having been appropriated and redistributed to

Mugabe's cronies who, having no idea how to run a farm, had simply sold off the machinery and left the ground to lie fallow.

Colonel Chang had been in Zimbabwe for a few years now. In fact he was amongst a group of the first "Military Advisors" to have been based in the country.

The Chinese government had decided to up their military involvement in Africa, despite all of their bleating to the contrary. One of the first things they had done, in a country that was crying out for doctors and farmers and teachers, had been to invest one hundred million dollars in a National Defense University to train soldiers. A meaningless white elephant that they handed over personally to the corrupt mister Mugabe.

Then they extended the country a bailout package in excess of twenty-seven billion dollars. Out of this package Mugabe himself appropriated a huge undisclosed amount.

In return the president gave the Chinese total control of the eight hundred-billion-dollar diamond mining paradise of Marange where they proceeded to set up the largest military base in Africa.

At the same time, they started negotiations to place military bases in Dijibouti. Nigeria, Algeria, Egypt, Congo, Mozambique, Angola and Zambia. "Advisors" and personal bodyguards were sent to all of these areas totaling some twenty thousand strong.

An old pastel blue Mazda 626 drove into view, dragging a massive red dust cloud behind in. The vehicle pulled up in front of the Fierce Dragon and two men got out.

Five ten, swarthy, short cropped hair. Both wore khaki clothes, cotton shirts, trousers and generic military issue boots. Shirts unbuttoned halfway down their torsos. Luxurious thatches of hair covered their chest.

Chang knew that they were Ukrainian. He knew that they were called Yarik & Igor. But even though he had been meeting like this for over two years, he still did not know who was who. Nor did he care.

They supplied him with rhino horn. He organized the horn to be flown to Hong Kong where it was received by Tai Zeng and that was all that colonel Chang was concerned with.

The Flying Tigers bailed out of their carriers and formed a large circle of steel around the vehicles.

Neither the Ukrainians or the Chinese greeted each other. Viktor walked around to the trunk of the Mazda, opened it, removed the spare tire and then opened a steel panel to reveal a false bottom. He dragged a large leather suitcase out and handed it to sergeant Feng.

It was heavy. At least seventy-five pounds. Perhaps a little more.

'Twelve horns,' said Viktor. 'One million dollars.'

Feng opened the case and checked. Then he clicked his fingers. One of his troops ran over. He carried a small, battery powered digital scale. Feng placed the case on the scale. Then he took a calculator out of his pocket and did a quick calculation. He glanced at the colonel and nodded.

Jin Chang took a small canvas pouch from his webbing and handed it to Viktor.

The Ukrainian accepted it and without checking, put it into his trouser pocket.

'Trust,' he said to the colonel. 'Something that you appear to be short of.'

Chang did not react. If he had been amongst other Chinese, such a gesture would have caused him a serious loss of face. But coming from these barbarians it was meaningless.

The poachers climbed back into their car, cranked the starter and drove off without a backward glance.

'Fucking hairy gorillas,' murmured the colonel.

Sergeant Feng scratched himself under his arms and did a passable imitation of a chimpanzee.

'Ook, ook, ook.'

Chang smiled.

Viktor glanced in his rear-view mirror and looked back at the Chinese. 'Christ, look at them,' he exclaimed. 'Fucking monkeys.'

Igor laughed out loud.

CHAPTER SIX

T hat morning, after Garrett told Petrus that he was coming with him, the chief presented them with a thirty-year-old Toyota Land Cruiser, a wad of dollars and a small cache of weapons including two antiquated AK47's, a Norinco, Chinese copy of a Colt 45, and some extra magazines and ammunition. All of the hardware was in atrocious condition. Rusted, dirty and coated in old oil. The cache was secreted into a false compartment under the RV, made up to look like part of the gas tank.

Petrus strapped on his customary Assegai in a sheath under his arm that allowed concealed carry.

It was then that the chief approached Garrett. He held a package in his one hand. It was wrapped in olive oilcloth.

Petrus nudged his friend in the ribs.

'Kneel,' he whispered under his breath.

Garrett immediately dropped to his knees and looked at the floor, showing the correct amount of re-spect.

'Stand,' commanded Petrus' father.

Garrett stood and the chief unwrapped the package and handed it to the soldier.

It was a two foot long, cold steel made machete. The handle had been bound in green ox hide and the blade had been hand engraved with the random geometric shapes of traditional Ndebele design. It was a magnificent weapon. Like Petrus' assegai, it too came with a shoulder rig.

Garrett fell to his knees again.

'Thank you, great one,' he said.

The chief smiled.

Next, the village *Sangoma*, or witchdoctor came to the fore. He flicked a viscous black liquid over both of the friends and then he took a bunch of herbs and barks and started to whip Garrett about the neck and shoulders, chanting as he did so.

Garrett grimaced in pain as the ancient witchdoctor whaled away at him, every hit leaving a raised red welt.

'It is a great honor,' encouraged Petrus. 'It will make you strong. Protect you from evil spirits.'

'When is it your turn?' asked the soldier.

'Already had it done,' answered Petrus.

'When?'

'Oh - long time ago.'

After another two minutes Garrett started to suspect that the *Sangoma* had simply taken an instant dislike to him and was simply taking the opportunity to smack him senseless with a bundle of twigs.

Finally, it stopped and the *Sangoma* spat in his hand, mixed the sputum with a pinch of brown powder and rubbed it into Garrett's hair.

Then, as one, everybody turned their backs on the two of them and walked away. There were no good-byes, no good lucks. Nothing.

It was as if they no longer existed.

'Wow,' said Garrett. 'Was it something I said?'

Petrus smiled. 'No. But until we avenge Malusi's murder we walk outside of the tribe. We are as ghosts.'

'Tough break,' said Garrett. 'Who's driving?'

'Me,' answered Petrus. 'I know where we're going. Sort of.'

'Cool,' said Garrett. 'Before we get going,' he continued. 'How did you manage to organize that machete so quickly. I only just told you that I was going to accompany you?'

Petrus said nothing but he had the good grace to look a little sheepish.

'You knew,' exclaimed Garrett. 'You knew that I would come with you.'

Petrus laughed. 'Of course. We are brothers. True?'

Garrett joined in with his laughter.

'True,' he affirmed.

Ten hours of hard driving and Garrett and Petrus were getting close to their destination. They were heading for Phalaborwa and had passed through towns with names as English as Ladysmith, Dundee and

Newcastle, Afrikaans names like Volksrust and Lydenburg and African names like eNtokozweni and Kwazanele.

The murder had taken place just below Makuleke and Garrett and Petrus had decided to follow the road from Makuleke until they found the actual site.

It was easy to find.

The landmine had torn a massive hole in the road. Four foot deep with a diameter of twenty feet across.

Shiny brass cartridges still littered the ground, even though it was a crime scene and the shells should have been collected as evidence.

Entire trees lay on the ground, shattered and stripped by the huge amount of firepower that had been laid down on the unsuspecting rangers.

With practiced sight both Garrett and Petrus relived the firefight. Noting where bodies had fallen and where the fire had come from.

Although literally gallons of blood had been shed during the fight, no sign of any stained the land. This was because any trace would have already been picked at by vultures or licked up by hyenas. In fact, the hyenas would even have swallowed any rocks and stones that had traces of blood on them.

Petrus stopped at the spot he deduced Malusi had been shot, and he stood and stared at the patch of ground. 'It was here,' he said.

Garrett cast his eyes about the scene, marking well where each body had fallen, then he agreed.

'Yes. It was there.'

Petrus knelt and wiped his hand across the parched earth on which his young brother had spilled his last life's-blood.

'Talk to me,' he whispered.

The dry air sighed softly across the land, stirring the grass and kicking up tiny puffs of red dust.

'Talk to me,' insisted Petrus.

High above them a flock of mossie sparrows flickered across the sky, abruptly changing direction as a Cape Vulture flew past them.

'Talk to me.'

And in the distance. Right on the very edge of hearing, a lion roared.

The Zulu warrior stood up and smiled.

'Let's go,' he said to Garrett. 'We need to find out who did this.'

B ravo Nyathi was fifteen years old. His father had died six weeks before in a car crash leaving behind his mother, Bravo and seven other siblings aged from three to twelve.

Bravo's mother worked in the town of Phalaborwa as a domestic servant. She stayed on the premises and managed to get home once or, if she was lucky, twice a month.

Whenever she did come home, she brought food. Dried beans, maize meal, salt and sugar. She also gave any extra money to Bravo's grandmother who took care of the family.

But try as she might, Bravo's mother could simply not earn enough to feed nine people and herself. And although granny tried her utmost, collecting worms and grubs to supplement their food, the family was slowly starving to death.

Bravo knew that steps had to be taken. And in a land where adulthood is oft thrust upon the young, he now accepted that he was the de facto man-of-the-house. As such he decided on a plan.

There were rumors of a man in a nearby village. A man that lived in the shadow of the law. A *tsotsi*. He went by the moniker of King Kentucky and he was both respected and feared by many, if not all.

It was said that The King was a man who offered good money for rhino horn. Bravo was unsure of what exact amounts of cash were involved. The rumor-mill had put about amounts as high as two thousand Rands. Some said even higher. Whatever it was - it was more than Bravo's mother brought home in a year of domestic servitude.

This rumor in itself meant would have meant little to the youthful head-of-the-house because, in reality, although he would have no problem breaking into the Kruger National Game Park, he would have no way of actually killing one of the huge pachyderms. But King Kentucky, who was a wily operator, did more than simply buy the horn. He also hired out rifles and ammunition to the prospective poachers.

That weekend Bravo's mother visited home. She stayed the night, gave granny her wad of savings, and left the next day, rushing so that she could get back to work early enough to be able to make her madam her Sunday dinner.

Bravo waited until everyone in the room was asleep and then, slowly and silently, he removed the meager wad of cash from under her pillow and he left, closing the door quietly behind him.

He knew that, without the money he had just taken, his family would not last beyond the week. But, although he felt nervous, he was confident that he would return within a couple of days bringing back untold wealth. A conquering hero.

He walked through the night, following directions he had gotten earlier that day. As the sun rose, he walked into the King's village. He needed no directions to the *tsotsi's* house. There was only one western-style abode in the village. A massive sprawling bungalow, painted in many bright colors, a roof of tin and glazed windows in every room.

Bravo walked up to the front door, squatted down and waited. He would never be so crass as to knock on the door or call out. King Kentucky was a man of great importance and, as such, it was up to him to deign to notice the young man. Bravo would simply wait for as long as that took.

After two hours the front door opened and a man stepped out. He was huge, four or five chins, bags of fat under his eyes, hands like over-inflated rubber gloves. Despite the already appalling Africa heat, he was dressed in a three-piece blue and silver pinstripe suit. Dark half-moons of sweat had already soaked through the underarms, edged with a rime of white salt. His face shone like it had been rubbed with cooking oil.

He stared at Bravo for a few seconds. The boy did not stand up. That would have been disrespectful.

'What do you want, *umfaan*, child?'

'I am not an *umfaan*,' said Bravo. 'I am a *madota*.'

The big man chuckled, the rumble of V8 engine. 'My mistake. So, *amadota*. What do you seek?'

'I seek King Kentucky. I wish to work for him.'

'Come with me.'

The man turned and walked back into the house. Bravo stood and followed. The inside of the house was cooler than the outside, but only marginally. They walked down a corridor, past many closed doors. Bravo could hear muted conversation behind some of them.

At the end of the corridor there was a set of double width doors. The big man opened them and entered. Once again, Bravo followed.

The room contained many books, lined up on the walls like a public library. There was a large wooden desk. Two chairs in front of it and one behind.

The big man went behind the desk and sat down.

'Right,' he said. 'Talk to me.'

'Are you the King?' asked Bravo.

'Some call me that,' admitted the big man. 'How can I help?'

'I want to hire a gun,' said Bravo.

The big man shook his head. 'No.'

'I have to,' insisted the boy. 'My family are starving. I need money.'

'I don't hire guns to children,' said the King. Before Bravo could argue the big man held his hand up. 'My word is final, boy. Do not anger me. If I rent you a gun, it will end in your death. Or maybe you will be arrested and then what? Personally, I don't care about you, but if the police get you then I am out by one gun. No. Leave.'

'I have money,' said Bravo, pulling the sheaf out and placing on the desk in front of the King.

'I have spoken,' commanded the big man. 'If you are so interested in a life of crime then start with a knife. Sneak into someone's house at night, cut their throat and take their money. That way is better. You don't need a gun.'

'I don't want to steal,' said Bravo. 'What would be the point? No one here has any money except for you and no one would steal from you.'

'Well then, why do you want a gun?'

'To kill the *obhejane*, the rhino.'

The King burst out laughing. 'You? Have you ever seen a rhino, boy?'

Bravo nodded. 'Plenty times. I live next to the fence at the Kruger Park. I know where all the holes in the fence are. Often, when I was younger, my friends and I would go into the park to look for Mopani worms and hunt birds. There I saw the rhino.'

The King stopped laughing and looked at the boy for a while. Solemn faced, intelligent, and desperate.

'So, you think that you could kill one and cut off its horn?'

'Yes,' affirmed Bravo.

The big man nodded. 'I think that you could,' he said. 'Wait.'

The King picked up a cell phone from his desk and dialed a number. Bravo could hear a phone ringing in another room in the vast rambling house.

'Sipho,' greeted the King. 'Bring me one of the old SKS rifles with five rounds of ammunition.' He looked up at Bravo. 'Would you like something to drink?'

The boy shrugged.

'Also, bring me a Castle beer and a can of Fanta Orange. Be quick.' He disconnected the call and placed the phone back on the desktop.

A mere few minutes later someone knocked on the door and then walked in. He came forward and laid down a rifle on the desktop. It was wrapped in a piece of sacking. Next to it he placed a bottle of Castle lager and an ice cold can of Fanta Orange.

The King slid the can across to Bravo. The boy popped the seal and took a long swallow. His eyes watered with pleasure as the sweet ice-cold soda fizzed down his throat. It was the first time that he had ever tasted a soda and, to him, it was the most luxurious experience of his life.

In that instant he vowed to himself that, when he had killed his rhino zerf King Kentucky had paid him, he would purchase an entire case of the bright orange pop and drink it all in one sitting.

The King picked up the old Russian SKS rifle and unwrapped the sacking. It was already loaded. Four rounds in the magazine and one in the chamber. Cocked and locked.

'Do you know how to work this?' he asked

Bravo shook his head. He had seen rifles before. AK 47's and bolt action hunting rifles but he had never actually held one.

'It's very simple,' said the big man. 'Inside there are five bullets. Don't worry about how they got there or such what, it doesn't concern you. This here is the trigger. You point the rifle at the rhino and pull the trigger. Each time you pull it the rifle will discharge one bullet. But before you do so you need to flick this small switch,' he indicated the safety. 'It must show this single dot here. Once you have done that it is good to go. Now, remember - you need to get close. As close as you can. Then you point at the rhino's head, preferably its eye, and pull the trigger until the bullets stop coming out. Okay? Then, when the rhino falls down you must take a knife and cut out its horn. Make sure that you cut deep, much of the horn is in the base. Do you have a big knife?'

Bravo nodded.

'Good.'

The King handed over the assault rifle. Bravo grunted as he took it. It was heavier than it looked.

'Now,' continued the King. 'Where do you live?'

Bravo told him.

'Good. You have three days to return with my rifle and my horn. If you do not come back within three days, I will send my men to come looking for you. You do not want that.'

'I will not let you down,' said Bravo.

'I know,' agreed King Kentucky as he pocketed the bundle of notes that Bravo had placed on the table.

'Now go,' he commanded as he threw the piece of sacking at Bravo. 'Wrap the weapon in that to conceal it. I will see you before three days is up.'

The boy bowed deeply and left the room.

CHAPTER EIGHT

Garrett and Petrus had simply consulted their map book and chosen the village that was closest to the point where Malusi had been ambushed. It seemed like a logical place to start their enquiries.

It was a mere fifteen-minute drive, and by the time they arrived the local headman was already waiting for them, having spotted the dust cloud from their vehicle some five minutes before.

They climbed out of the cab and stretched, popping joints and groaning at stiff muscles.

The headman approached.

'Welcome, strangers,' he said as he walked towards them.

Garrett looked up and was surprised to see the man do a visible double take as he saw Petrus. He was even more surprised when the headman immediately prostrated himself on the ground in front of the Zulu prince.

'Baba,' he said. 'I cannot express my happiness at seeing your countenance once again. Truly, we all believed that you were dead.'

'Yeah well, apparently not,' said Petrus. 'Stand, old one. I come in peace, simply looking for information. Relax.'

'I see that one of us commands a little respect around here,' said Garrett.

Petrus grinned wryly. 'Yep. Probably got me mixed up with someone else. It happens a lot.'

The headman stood and beckoned them to follow him. As he walked, he called for people, shouting out a string of instructions as they arrived to his calls. By the time they arrived at his hut, beer was already being brought and fires were been started.

The plaintive bleating of a goat could be heard as the villagers prepared it for slaughter.

Three small stools were placed outside the entrance to the headman's hut and small beerpots were offered.

Petrus lifted his pot, downed it in one mighty draft and smacked his lips loudly in appreciation. Taking his lead from him, Garrett proceeded to do the same.

The headman grinned and nodded, well pleased at their obvious enjoyment of his proffered refreshments.

Within minutes a platter of sliced goat meat arrived, prepared with the speed and skill of a master butcher. The chief scattered a liberal handful of salt onto it and threw it straight onto the fire. It sizzled and spat and smoked. The fat melted and ran into the flames causing them to flare up in an orgy of heat.

Using his bare hands, the chief flicked the charred slabs of meat from the fire and flicked them onto the wooden platter.

They ate without cutlery, using their teeth to saw through the tough, fragrant salted meat.

The strong gamey taste went perfectly with the tart African beer and Garrett ate his fill with genuine pleasure.

After they had eaten Garrett produced a pack of Gauloise and offered the headman and then Petrus. They all sat in silence for a while before they spoke and, when they finally did, it was as custom dictated, initially about inconsequentialities. Weather, crops, cattle. The state of the youth. Petrus' father's health.

Finally, Petrus deemed that it was time to discuss the real reasons that they were there.

Petrus told of his brother's murder and the resultant charge of vengeance that had been laid on him.

Then he leaned forward and lowered his voice so that the headman had to lean towards him to hear.

'I need to know who did this,' he said.

The headman looked nervous. 'It had nothing to do with me or my people,' he said.

Petrus nodded. 'I know that,' he said. His voice now a sibilant whisper. 'If I even slightly suspected that you were involved, even now your family would be weeping over your corpse as their houses burned to the ground.'

The headman shuddered. 'There are many bad men around here. And many could have been involved. But if I had to name one person who would know I would say; The General.'

'The General,' repeated Petrus.

'Yes. He is a youngster. One of the new breed. Doesn't respect the old ways, thinks that he's an American. Wears gold jewelry, sunglasses, tracksuits. Runs a village up North. He works with some white men. Foreigners. He provides local muscle. Trackers. Information. They go into the Kruger with the white men and kill the *obhejane*. Also, they kill anyone who tries to stop them. Even anyone who refuses to work for them. He tells everyone that he is ex-Umkontowisiswe, ANC freedom fighter. But he is a liar. He is too young to have taken part in the struggle. Maybe he has had some military training because he runs the village like an army base.'

'Exactly where is this village?' asked Petrus. 'I think that this so called general and I need to talk.'

'Stay the night, baba,' answered the headman. 'Tomorrow I will provide you with a guide. He will take you there.'

Petrus glanced at Garrett who nodded his agreement. It was running late and it would be better to start with a new sun. The prince nodded his affirmation and the headman clapped his hands to attract attention. One of the girls skipped over and he commanded that she prepare a hut for the guests.

They were shown to a hut situated two away from the headman's abode. Obviously, someone had been turned out of their house and relegated to another dwelling to make space for the honored guest. It was a simple round room. Carpets covered the bare earth and two sleeping mats were laid out on the top of the carpets. At the head of each sleeping mat was a traditional Zulu wooden headrest in lieu of a pillow. A pump-up paraffin lamp sat in the middle of the room and provided a bright orange-yellow light that filled the room.

There was a bowl of water, two facecloths and two small pots of beer.

Both Garrett and Petrus nodded their thanks and placed their kit next to the bedrolls.

Garrett sat cross-legged and immediately started to strip the weapons that they had been given, laying the separate parts of the AK47's out in front of him on the carpets and then thoroughly cleaning each part with one of the facecloths. He whistled tunelessly through his teeth as he did so, his mind free of thought as his body carried out a task that was so familiar to as to be almost an autonomous action.

Petrus sharpened his already razor-sharp assegai. The sound a chilling rasp of stone on steel as he drew it across the blade. The orange-yellow lamplight shone off the sliver of sharpened blade and reflected back, turning it into a blade of fire. Like a weapon of legend, forged from the very flames of hell itself.

There was a tentative knock at the entrance and a young girl let herself in. She was perhaps sixteen or seventeen. Buxom and healthy with firm round buttocks and a generous bosom. She wore a short skirt. The top half of her body was unadorned apart from two or three bead necklaces.

She bowed deeply to Petrus, her eyes downcast. 'I have been sent to warm your sleeping mat, my lord,' she said.

Petrus grinned.

Garrett raised an eyebrow.

'Thank you, pretty one,' responded Petrus. 'But tonight, I think that I will refrain.'

The girl raised her eyes and looked directly at the prince. 'My lord does not find me attractive?'

Petrus laughed. 'Far from it, my beauty. But tonight, is a night for contemplation. Thank the headman. Tell him that I was appreciative but I am…tired.'

The girl nodded and left the hut, backing away until she had passed through the low entrance.

'Cradle robber,' quipped Garrett with a grin.

'What's that mean?' asked Petrus.

'It's an expression we whiteys use to describe an older man who goes for young girls.'

'But I turned her down.'

'That's true,' declared Garrett.

'Anyway,' continued Petrus. 'You're just jealous.'

'Also true,' admitted the soldier.

The two of them laughed and then continued to prepare their tools of death.

The next morning, they rose early, beating the sun by some twenty minutes. The headman was already up and about and his girls had prepared a breakfast of well-salted thick maize porridge for the two guests. He had also ensured that the Landcruiser had been topped up with diesel from his own supply and he had commanded a troop of *umfaans* to clean and polish the vehicle.

Its aged, dented bodywork glowed in the rising sun like an old Hollywood actress who had undergone far too much plastic surgery. An attempt to cover age with the manufactured gloss of false youth.

Next to the newly buffed vehicle stood a man. He had a threadbare blanket wrapped around his scrawny shoulders. His beard and the hair on his head were as white as a Himalayan snowcap.

He saw Garrett and Petrus approaching and he gave them a smile and raised his assegai in salute. His mouth as toothless as a clam. But Garrett noticed that his assegai was bright and clean, the blade freshly oiled and the edges shone like newly minted silver.

'That is your guide,' explained the headman.

'He appears to be rather well advanced, age wise,' commented Garrett. 'Are you sure that he's up to the task?'

The headman looked at Garrett in puzzlement, then he continued. 'His name is Winstonchurchill. He is very wise.'

Petrus said nothing, but Garrett wondered if the ancient old man would be more hindrance than help.

'I only hope that he stays alive until we get there,' he mumbled under his breath as he climbed into the passenger seat.

Petrus got behind the wheel and Winstonchurchill hopped into the back seats, moving like an arthritic stork.

The guide pointed ahead, showing them the direction that they were to head. Petrus waved a final goodbye to the headman, cranked the engine into life and stepped on the gas.

'How far away?' asked Garrett of their guide.

The old man shrugged.

'Great,' said Garrett. 'A guide who doesn't know anything.'

The old man stared at Garrett for a while, his dark eyes boring into him as he did so.

'I know much, *Isosha,*' he said. 'Even though I have just met you, I already know your true identity. I know your life. I know your dreams.'

'Yeah, whatever,' said Garrett, feeling uncomfortable under the old man's scrutiny.

'You run, young *Isosha.* You try to hide. But you cannot, for the thing that you run from is inside you. You try to run from yourself. And you say I know nothing. Even the most inept herd boy knows that you cannot escape yourself. You live in a land far away and you serve the king of the mountains. You are his...' he paused for a while as he thought. 'You are the keeper of his cattle, his lands.'

The old man sniffed in disapproval of Garrett's crass behavior.

'And as for your question. I have traveled to the general's village before, but never have I have traveled there in a motorcar. It is a long walk. Eight or nine hours. In a car...who knows? Shorter, definitely. But how much shorter I do not know.'

Petrus chuckled. 'Consider yourself owned, my friend,' he said.

Garrett nodded. 'I am sorry, Winstonchurchill. I was impolite. I apologize.'

The old man shrugged. 'It is of no moment. You are too young to know any better.'

Garrett said nothing. There was nothing to say.

The Landcruiser ground on through the African heat, dragging a dust cloud behind it as it ate up the miles.

CHAPTER NINE

The Chinese ambassador to Zimbabwe, Mister Lin Chun glanced across the banquet table and caught the eye of senior colonel Zhao Yuan. Although neither of them showed any outward emotion, the ambassador knew exactly what the senior colonel was thinking.

Almost in exact concert, the ambassador and the colonel swiveled to look at the guests of honor. The two guests were the reason that the Chinese government was spending such a stupendous amount of money on yet another embassy banquet.

Grace and Robert Mugabe.

And if the ambassador were honest with himself, he would admit that the banquet was truly being thrown to curry favor with Mugabe's forty-four-year-old wife, as opposed to the demented ninety-one-year-old president. This was because everyone knew that Grace, formally a girl in the president's typing pool, was the de facto next in command. In actual fact, the reins of power already lay in her grasp as, to all intents and purposes, Robert had already gone bye-bye, retaining as much grasp on reality as a nine-year-old on crack.

The menu was designed to impress…and it was not an easy task to impress "Gucci" Grace, a woman who used to spend upwards of ten million dollars a day on shopping sprees in London, before the UK government banned both her and Robert from entering the country.

Conspicuous consumption took on an entirely different meaning to someone who owned over a thousand pairs of Ferrigamo and Gucci shoes, each costing more than five years earnings of the average Zimbabwean, whose taxes were actually paying for the outrageously expensive footwear. When the press had once questioned her about her penchant for high-priced designer footwear, she had told them that she had very narrow feet so it was imperative that she had her shoes hand made for her.

As it happened, the female dictator-in-waiting did not even seem to notice the quality of the food.

She had hurriedly spooned down the Red Bird Nest Soup, a glutinous broth consisting mainly of the most expensive bird spit in the world, and then she had wiped her bowl with a hunk of bread, like a starving peasant seeking to clean the last bit of available nutrient from their plate.

The next course was Abalone. A shellfish that had been illegally harvested off the Cape of Good Hope in South Africa. Grace pushed it away with a look of distaste announcing that she did not like fish.

The Kobe beef with Matsutake mushrooms and white truffles went down better, although she did send it back to be re-cooked, reducing the tender cuts of the world's most expensive beef into something akin to jerky.

The meal ended with trays of Chocopologie chocolates.

The final bill ran in at over ten thousand dollars a head, excluding the copious amounts of alcohol being consumed.

Whilst the coffee was being served, Robert Mugabe decided to regale all with his current thoughts on homosexuality, a subject that he had lately become totally obsessed with.

'That Obama,' he stated. 'He wants us to embrace homosexuality. I say No. John and John - no. Maria and Maria - no. They are worse than dogs or pigs. Worse. I own pigs and even they know the difference between male and female. We will cut their heads off. That is why China is our friend - they do not insist that we become anal vilifiers.'

He wiped his sweating face with a table napkin and continued.

'And that David Cameron with his little pink nose. He must keep out of our face. England is simply a cold uninhabitable country with small houses and homosexuals. I told them; when they sent food to us, I told them, take your food away. We have enough food. What are you trying to do? Choke us? Why foist this food upon us. I told them and I burned all the food they sent.'

Abruptly he burped and fell instantly asleep, snoring softly, his ancient head resting on his chest.

Ambassador Lin Chun noticed Grace looking at the president with barely veiled contempt, and then she continued to flirt outrageously with her bodyguard, licking her spoon and batting her eyelids.

Lin Chun found her to be utterly ridiculous but he was not surprised. It was well known that she constantly had a string of affairs or dalliances. It was also assumed that, on the demise of Robert, she would assume power and appoint Gideon Gono, ex head of the reserve bank, as her number two. She had been caught, some years before, having a very public affair with Gideon. The then head of the reserve bank had gone into hiding to escape the wrath of Robert. But nowadays the old man was so far gone that he didn't seem to remember, let alone care.

So, the dictator slept on.

And his wife continued flirting with the help.

And the Chinese ambassador smiled and smiled and smiled until his face ached.

CHAPTER TEN

Bravo had entered the Kruger National Park through a hole in the fence on the west side of the reserve.

The boy had walked all day and into the night and had arrived at the perimeter at about half past midnight. Then he had found a thick copse of bush and slept under it, totally worn out from his trek. Waking before the sun, he found a hole in the fence and proceeded into the reserve, searching for rhino tracks.

Now, fourteen hours later, with the sun once more about to set, he was utterly and completely lost.

He had no idea where the fence was, no idea what direction he had come from and no idea where he was going. He drank the last of his water from an old soda bottle that he had filled at the start of his trek. The water was as warm as tea and seemed to evaporate before it even got to the bottom of his parched throat.

It was then that he heard it. A low coughing grunt. Atavistic and primeval. A sound that is guaranteed to make even the hardest man shiver with dread.

The sound of the male lion.

Terror gripped Bravo with ice-cold fingers. Suddenly the antiquated rifle in his hands that had previously felt heavy and solid now felt vague and insubstantial. No longer a weapon and now simply a lump of wood and steel.

It was one thing to contemplate shooting a rhino. A large, shortsighted slow-witted herbivore that would usually retreat before it considered attack. It was a completely different ball game to taking on a full-grown male lion. Half a ton of carnivorous feline aggression that had evolved to become the apex predator in land that spawned predators like a ghetto spawned gang members.

Bravo ran towards the closest substantial looking thorn tree and climbed it as fast as he could, finally nestling in a crook high above the ground. Safe. For the moment.

He never saw the lion but he heard it as it prowled the veld around him. Eventually he fell asleep whilst clinging to the branch, driven to slumber by utter exhaustion brought on by physical exercise, fear and dehydration.

The next morning a ray of sunlight stabbed through his eyelids and jerked him awake. He took a second to work out where he was and then he frantically scanned the surrounding area for the lion.

There was no lion but there was, to his absolute joy and amazement, a lone rhino. It stood below the thorn tree. Unmoving. A large gray statue, crudely molded out of child's clay.

With shaking hands, he pointed the rifle. Squinting down the barrel, lining the steel sights up with the rhino's head.

He pulled the trigger.

Nothing happened.

In panic he pulled the trigger again, squeezing as hard as he can.

Still nothing.

Then he remembered King Kentucky's instructions. Flick the small switch. Bravo fumbled at the lever and pushed it with his thumb. Inadvertently slipping it from "safe" past "single shot" and onto "automatic fire".

Once again, he lined the rifle up. Aimed and pulled the trigger. The assault rifle disgorged all five rounds in under a second as it cycled on full automatic fire. The weapon flew from Bravo's hands and fell to the ground. At the same time the recoil knocked the boy from his perch and he followed the rifle down, banging into the branches on the way down, slamming head first into the sunbaked, rock-hard soil and rendering him unconscious.

He came to half an hour later. His tongue felt swollen and dry. His head throbbed and his mouth tasted of blood. Metallic. Smokey.

He glanced up to see the rhino's head, also lying on the ground, only three feet away from him.

He screamed and rolled away before realizing that the huge creature was dead.

Amazed that he had actually killed it, Bravo stood up, walked to the animal and gingerly touched its flank. There was no reaction. He looked more closely at its head. Three of the 7.62mm rounds had struck the rhino in the face. One in its eye, the other entering its temple and the third tearing a furrow along the side of its magnificent main horn.

Bravo pulled his knife from his belt and immediately started to cut into the flesh below the horn.

Three hours later he placed the bloody horn into a black plastic rubbish bag. His fingers were raw with broken blisters and his once sharp knife was a dull as a wooden ruler. But he was a wealthy man. In a little over two days, he had earned a year's worth of wages. His family would live and, if he did this only two or three times a year, they could all live in comparative luxury.

He stood up slowly, like an old man, tortured muscles straining in pain. Rubbing his eyes with the back of his hands and closing them tightly for a while, he tried to create some moisture so that he would be able to blink away the red dust that was scratching at his pupils.

Bravo never saw the blow that hit him in the side of his face, shattering his lower jaw, knocking out four of his teeth and hammering him to the ground.

Whimpering in pain he looked up from his prostrate position. For some reason he could no longer see in color. The world presented itself in grays and blacks and whites. And it was all badly out of focus.

A white man stood over him. Not tall, maybe five foot ten. Close cropped black hair. Unshaven. His shirt open to reveal a massively hirsute chest. His arms were covered in tattoos.

'Hey, boy,' he said. 'Are you alone?'

Bravo nodded.

'This your rhino?'

Another nod.

'You kill this rhino by yourself?'

Again, the boy nodded in affirmation.

'Well done,' said the man.

Despite the pain, Bravo allowed himself a tiny smile of pride.

The man shot him twice in the face.

'Now it's my rhino,' said Igor.

Behind him both Yarik and Stas laughed.

That Igor was one funny guy.

CHAPTER ELEVEN

They stopped a mile away from the general's village, traveling the rest of the way on foot. From the cover of the surrounding bush, Garrett raised a pair of binoculars to his eyes and scanned the village.

'What do you see?' whispered Petrus.

'A village. Seems to be some sort of perimeter fence, although it's really badly kept. Fallen over in some places. Guards. Patrolling in singles. Three of them. One smoking. Armed with shotguns.'

The soldier handed the binoculars to Petrus. 'Here, take a look for yourself. I'll tell you something for nothing, though. If this guy fancies himself as some sort of military leader, then he must be the shittest officer in the world. The place is a bloody side show.'

'I agree,' affirmed Petrus. 'I reckon that we simply wait until nightfall, go in, grab the general and ask him some questions.'

'Why not,' said Garrett. 'No need to complicate things. Especially when the place is such a joke like this is.'

Winstonchurchill also nodded his agreement, even though he had nothing at all to do with the decision-making process.

The three of them retreated back into the thick bush, backtracking for five hundred yards. There they stopped, made themselves comfortable, lit cigarettes and settled down to wait for nightfall.

Hours later, at two o'clock in the morning, by the graveyard glimmer of the new moon, Garrett and Petrus snuck into the village. Much to his disgust they had left Winstonchurchill at the perimeter to keep a look out. He brandished his assegai above his head as he insisted that he wanted to go in with them, but Petrus command him to stay. Eventually he bowed and acceded to the prince's authority.

The two friends ghosted through the village. They moved without sound, carrying only bladed weapons, more like shades than men. A leopard and a panther.

The general's house was easy to find. It was at the top of the village and, painted in black script above the front door was a sign that read, "The General".

Petrus looked at the sign and shook his head.

'What a dick,' he whispered to Garrett.

There was no guard at the door but it was locked. Garrett simply slid the blade of his machete along the doorjamb and pushed the latch back, easing the door open at the same time.

They entered and closed the door quietly behind them.

The entrance led directly into a large sitting room area. A corridor ran off the sitting room. There were two doors in the corridor. One was already open. Garrett looked inside. A bedroom. Double bed. Empty.

Petrus took hold of the handle to the second door and twisted. It was unlocked and the door opened smoothly and silently. They shut it behind them.

A young man lay asleep in the bed. He was alone.

Petrus walked over, put his hand over the man's mouth and then slapped him hard across the face.

The man went apoplectic, thrashing and flailing about as he woke. But Petrus held him down with a grip of iron and his hand prevented the man from yelling out. Eventually the man stopped struggling.

'Good,' said Petrus. 'Now listen and listen very carefully, your life depends on it.' He drew out his assegai with his free hand and held it in front of the general's face. 'I need to ask you some questions. In order to answer you will need to speak. So, I am going to remove my hand from your mouth. If you shout or scream, I will take this blade and stick it in your eye. Do you understand?'

The general nodded.

'Do you believe me?'

He nodded again.

'Excellent,' said Petrus as he lifted his hand from the man's mouth.

'I know who you are,' said the general, his voice harsh with fear. 'You are the mad prince.'

'Good,' said Petrus. 'That will save us introducing ourselves. Now, boy, we don't have much time so listen and then answer. A couple of weeks ago, a convoy of game rangers were ambushed in the Kruger Park. They were all killed, their cargo of rhinos was destroyed and their horns removed. I need to know if you, or your men were involved.'

'I don't know anything about that,' said the general.

Without warning Petrus punched him in the nose. It broke with a soft crunch.

'Think harder,' he said.

The general shrank back, attempting to force his body deeper into his mattress in an effort to distance himself from the hard man standing over him.

At the same time the door burst open and a man ran in brandishing an AK47.

'Don't move,' he shouted. 'Still. Everybody stand still.'

'Oh, great,' said Petrus as he turned towards Garrett. 'How come you didn't hear him coming?'

'How come you didn't?' retaliated the soldier.

'I was busy interrogating dickhead here,' countered Petrus.

'Shut up, shut up,' screamed the newcomer with the AK.

Both Garrett and Petrus turned to look at him.

He waved the barrel of the assault rifle at the two of them; his hands were shaking, his eyes darting from side to side.

Then, without warning, he stiffened and looked down at his chest. A foot of blood covered bright steel had magically appeared there. It disappeared with an obscene sucking sound as it was withdrawn.

The man fell forward, dead before he hit the floor and Winstonchurchil stepped over him and into the room, his face split by a wide toothless grin.

The old man waved his bloody assegai above his head. 'I stab him,' he said.

'Yes,' agreed Garrett. 'You certainly did.'

'Like the old days,' the ancient enthused as he thrust his assegai into the air in front of him. 'Just like the old days.' He walked over to the general who was still lying on his bed, his eyes wide in horror. 'Who is this? ' he asked, as he poked at him with his spear, inadvertently sinking the blade inch deep into the prostrate general.

'Hey, fuck off, old man,' he shouted. 'He's stabbing me. Tell him to stop,' he appealed to Petrus.

'Tell me what I need to know,' said Petrus. 'If not, then I'll let this old man keep stabbing you until you die. Eventually.'

'Okay. Look, it wasn't my boys or me. It was a foreigner. A Russian, I think. I don't know his name. He has his own men, uses us for local info only. We help him to track the rhino, we know which rangers are susceptible to a bribe, keep watch on the fences. The Russian pays well. But we don't actually kill the rhino. His men do.'

'Where is he based?'

'I don't know. Genuinely. Probably Johannesburg. That's all that I know. Please. Tell the old man to fuck off now.'

Petrus looked at Garrett.

Garrett nodded. 'I reckon that he's telling the truth.'

'I agree,' said Petrus.

'But?' asked Garrett.

Petrus shrugged. 'In some way he is responsible for Malusi's death. If he is, well then, he must die.'

'And if he isn't?' asked Garrett.

Petrus shrugged again.

Behind them the general gave an abrupt squeal that was cut short by a gurgling sound. They spun around to see Winstonchurchill wiping the blade of his assegai clean on the general's bed sheets.

'I stab him,' the old man said, his face still agrin.

'Jesus Christ,' said Garrett. 'You blood thirsty, mad old bastard.'

Winstonchurchill nodded in agreement. 'Yes,' he said.

The three of them slipped out of the unsuspecting village, leaving it sleeping and without leadership.

CHAPTER TWELVE

Solomon Nagedi was tired. A deep, visceral fatigue. An exhaustion not only of the body but also the soul.

He had been a game ranger at the Kruger National Park for twelve years now. He was married. He had two young sons. His wife also worked for the game park. She was a cleaner for the tourist chalets in the reserve. The four of them lived in quarters provided to them by the parks commission. The place was clean and had running water and electricity. It was small, actually meant only for single male occupancy, but Solomon was happy. His wife and he slept in the bedroom and the two boys slept in the living-come-kitchen-eating area.

Twelve years ago, when Solomon had first joined up, he had loved his job. He showed tourists the wonders of the African bush. He kept the fences to the reserve intact, he was involved with animal research and conservation and every day he returned home feeling as though he had achieved something.

For the first three years not one rhino had died from poaching. And then, nine years ago, two of the huge, gentle beasts had been killed. He still remembered the shock that he had felt when he came upon the scene. The dead bodies, the horribly mutilated faces. The sadness.

The next year twenty were taken.

And then thirty. Fifty. Sixty.

Last year almost one thousand two hundred rhinos had been destroyed by man's greed.

The first game ranger had been killed by poachers in 2009. Now they lost up to one every single week.

Solomon had been in nineteen firefights in the last two years. Six of his compatriots had been killed. Solomon himself had shot and killed two poachers.

In the last twelve months the game ranger had seen more action than the average veteran of the entire Afghanistan or Iraqi wars.

And he had received no military training whatsoever.

So, although it was unusual for him, Solomon decided to have a beer at the local bar before he went home. He wanted, just a few minutes by himself. Time to let the cogs of his brain run free, lubricated by a couple of ice-cold lagers.

After his second solitary beer another appeared, unordered, at his elbow, followed closely by a stranger.

The newcomer was about the same height as Solomon. He wore good quality, khaki cotton trousers and a matching shirt. His shirt was unbuttoned to his lower chest, revealing a gold medallion nestled amongst a thatch of black hair. His arms were covered with tattoos.

He offered his hand. 'My name is Igor.'

Solomon took it without enthusiasm. He wanted to be alone.

'Solomon.'

'So,' continued Igor, looking at Solomon's uniform. 'You are with the parks board.'

The ranger nodded.

'Listen, Solomon,' said Igor, as he pulled his chair closer, creating a sense of privacy. 'I would like to make you an offer.'

'I'm not looking for insurance and I'm too poor to invest any money,' said Solomon.

Igor chuckled. 'No, my friend. I don't want you to invest in me, I want to invest in you.'

'I'm listening.'

'I have been taking some notice of you. I note that you spend a lot of time in the field. Very hands on, as it were.'

Solomon nodded. 'Correct.'

'Well, we are looking for a partner. Someone to work with us in an advisory capacity. We are willing to pay a small retainer, shall we say two hundred dollars a month as well as a commission on results.'

'What results?' Asked Solomon.

'Profitable results,' countered the Ukrainian.

'What was your name again?'

'Igor.'

'Okay, Igor. I'm tired, I want to finish my beer and go home. Get to the point.'

Igor slid a cell phone across the bar top. Cheap. Used. 'This has been pre-programmed with my number,' he said. 'All that you do is tell me when you come across any rhino spoor. Where it is, how many, how fresh. That's all. For that you get two hundred American every month and a bonus of five hundred American for each confirmed shipment.'

'Confirmed shipment?'

'Every horn that we get.'

Solomon downed his beer and sighed. 'Go away, Igor.'

'It's a good offer,' insisted the Ukrainian.

'Just fuck off, Igor. I won't report this to anyone. I won't talk about it. Just leave me alone.'

'Why?' insisted Igor. 'Do you honestly love rhinos that much. Are you really so enamored with your job that you would give up the opportunity to quadruple your salary?'

Solomon shook his head. 'To be honest, Igor,' he said. 'I can't fucking stand rhinos anymore. No animal is worth the human lives that we have lost. I hate my job. I hate that I have no choice but to stay with it or starve. I hate the fear that I have to live with every fucking day that we go out on patrol. But even more than that - I hate people like you. You come in here with your dollars and try to buy me. Well, I am not for sale.

I may hate my job. I may hate my life but it is mine to hate. So, fuck you, Igor. Fuck you very much.'

Igor face twisted into a mask of barely controlled anger. 'You misunderstand me, Solomon,' he rasped. 'This is not a negotiation.' He slapped two hundred dollars onto the bar top. Ten crisp twenty dollar notes. 'Your first payment. Now, you work for me.'

Solomon picked up the money and threw it in Igor's face.

The Ukrainian left the bar. He did not look back. He did not pick up the money.

Solomon decided to order another beer. He needed it.

The next morning the local fire chief deduced that the fire that had burned down Solomon's dwelling that night was due to an electrical fault. The coroner picked up the four bodies, an adult male, an adult female and two pre-pubescent boys. There was no autopsy. There was no investigation.

The fire chief spent his five-hundred-dollar bonus on a flat screen television complete with surround sound.

CHAPTER THIRTEEN

T hey took Winstonchurchill back to his village, thanked him and the headman and then left. As they drove off, they could see Winstonchurchill in the rear-view mirror. It was easily apparent that he had already started to regale the people with a tale of his exploits as he jumped up and down and stabbed the air with his assegai. Both Garrett and Petrus smiled.

The pickup droned back towards Johannesburg. Garrett drove whilst Petrus gave directions. The Zulu spent much of the time, during their long return trip, on his cell, making enquiries.

The General told them that the Russian was responsible for Malusi's death, but that did not do a lot to narrow the field. According to the many people that Petrus contacted, there were many Russians involved in shady dealings in the Johannesburg area.

Eventually Petrus made a call to someone called Jovito. Now they were heading to meet with him at his home in Diepsloot.

Diepsloot was an informal settlement consisting of around two hundred thousand people. The chosen method of construction seemed to consist mainly of corrugated iron sheets and cardboard.

Just before they arrived at Diepsloot, they drove past Dainfern. A fully fenced golf and living estate, complete with its own armed guards, private school, restaurants and shops. An oasis of beauty within sight of Diepsloot. Ten-million-dollar houses almost side by side with two-dollar shacks. Putting greens and water fountains as opposed to bare earth and raw sewage.

'So, who are we going to see?' asked Garrett.

'His name is Jovito. He's an amagent. A gangster. But be careful,' continued Petrus. 'These guys are as touchy as all hell. And don't be shocked at how young they all are. By definition an amagent is a youngster. They're basically the new flavor of gangster. Chip on the shoulder, hard upbringing, violent and proud of it.'

'Is that why you kept the AK's out?'

Petrus nodded. 'With these boys you go large or you go home. It's all about image, so be cool.'

Following Petrus' instructions, Garrett threaded the Land Cruiser through the narrow streets, almost brushing the walls of the makeshift shacks as they crawled through the township.

Eventually Petrus called a stop.

Garrett pulled up next to a dwelling that was noticeably more substantial than those around it.

Brick and plywood walls, corrugated roof. A fence. A gate. Standing at the gate were two young boys, no more than fourteen or fifteen. Both had baseball caps on backwards, Nike trainers, Pierre Cardin jeans and shirts.

They were both openly armed. One with a Skorpion machine pistol and the other with a chrome plated Colt 357 magnum.

They stared aggressively at the Land Cruiser until Petrus climbed out. Then their expressions both changed from belligerent to respectful.

'Gentlemen,' he greeted them.

'*Baba*, father,' they greeted back.

'Here to see Jovito.'

The smaller boy carrying the Colt opened the gate and beckoned for them to follow him.

'You can leave the car,' he said. 'We will watch it.'

The two followed him into the house. It was obvious that the dwelling had started off as a one-room shack and then had been simply added onto whenever the need for more space arose.

There were no corridors as rooms were simply attached to rooms. Many of them were completely interior with no outside windows or natural lighting.

A reek of smoke and marijuana permeated the place, sweet and woody.

The room that they were heading for was at the back of the house. Large, square. The windows covered with dark drapes. Nineteen seventies style leather furniture filled the room. Dirty cream, overstuffed. On the floor a shag-pile carpet. Also a murky shade of dairy.

A neon sign graced the entire side of one wall. The word, "Cocktails" in blue with a yellow martini glass and a red olive. The olive flashed on and off in the glass like a warning beacon. Perhaps it was a cherry.

A mirror ball spun slowly in the middle of the ceiling, filling the space with a snowfall of flickering lights. The entire ensemble was finished off with a huge fish tank in the one corner.

When Garrett looked closely at it, it was immediately apparent that the orange fish inside were all plastic fakes. Bobbing to the surface and then sinking back down as the air pump picked them up and then dropped them in an endless cycle of ersatz existence.

Gangster rap was pumping through a pyramid of speakers, the volume low but the bass setting so high that the music was felt on a visceral level, as opposed to an aural one.

The whole scenario gave Garrett an instant headache.

There were six boys sitting on the sofas. One of the youngsters stood up and walked over to Petrus. They shook hands, reversing grips in the African way.

Petrus turned to Garrett.

'Jovito, Garrett. Garrett, leader of the local amagents, Jovito.'

The two shook hands.

'Come,' said Jovito. 'Sit. We talk.'

'First turn this shit off,' said Petrus, pointing at the music system.

Jovito laughed and clicked his fingers. One of the youths turned the music off. Then he pulled out a packet of Rothmans cigarettes and offered. Both Garrett and Petrus accepted and the amagent lit. A gold Dunhill lighter.

'How can I help you, *baba*?'

Petrus told the young gangster about Malusi's death, the rhinos and the Russian connection.

Jovito listed carefully and then he sat in silence for a while. Finally, he spoke.

'I need to see some people, *baba*. Please stay here. I will be back in a few minutes.' He pointed at another youth in the room. 'This is Pulani. He is my second. If you want anything, food, drink, dagga, tell him and he will get it.'

Petrus nodded.

Jovito left the room, already dialing out on his cell.

Garrett took out his pack of Gauloise' and offered them around. Pulani and one other youngster accepted, as did Petrus. They all lit their own.

'I have heard of you,' said Pulani to Garrett. 'You are the white man who is possessed by demons.'

Garrett stared at the gangster for a while, his face expressionless. Then he spoke.

'How old are you, Pulani?'

'I am fifteen.'

'Young.'

Pulani shrugged. 'Jovito is seventeen and he is the boss-man.' He pointed at another boy. 'Jabulai there, he is thirteen and he has already killed twice. We are as old as we are.'

'So how did you get into this?'

'I grew up without clothes. I was wearing my sister's dresses without any underwear. When I was young my mother was working for a white lady and she used to tell me how her dishes were not put at the same place as her madam's dishes. They were put with the dog's dishes. It simply means a black man is a dog. When my uncle died, we didn't slaughter a cow because we didn't have money. We bought the meat at the butchery. I was young but I do remember other people were laughing at us. Then. One day, when someone laughed, I took a knife and I poked it in his eye. He didn't laugh any-more. Jovito saw me do it and he asked if I wanted to work with him. Together we used our knives to steal some guns. Then money and more guns. If anybody laughed at us we killed them. Now we are genuine amagents. We have respect. We are leaders of men.'

'And Jovito? What's his story?'

'His father left for another women when he was two. When he was nine his mother died and he moved in with his father and seven stepbrothers and sisters. He had to sleep outside the front door and when his father was at work, he wasn't allowed in the house at all. He had no school uniform so was not allowed to attend the local school. When he was twelve, he stabbed his old-est stepbrother over an altercation about his mother. He had to leave and fend for himself. He was strong and showed no mercy. Now he is the big man around here. Also, he knows Petrus, so people fear him even as they fear Petrus.'

'Why?' asked Garrett. 'Is Petrus also possessed by demons?'

Pulani shook his head. 'No. Only you are. People fear Petrus because they say that he cannot be killed. Many have tried. He has been shot and stabbed countless times. Others say that he is dead already.'

'What do you believe?' asked Garrett.

Pulani shrugged. 'I think that it does not matter either way. All know that, if you even try to kill Petrus, then his father will bring his impis and that will be the end.'

'Fair enough,' admitted Garrett. 'I think that you are probably right.'

Before Petrus could comment Jovito walked back into the room.

'Talk to me,' said Petrus.

'There are many so called Russians,' answered Jovito. 'Some are Russian, others are Croatian, Serbian, Ukrainians. The people call them all Russians. Then, of course, there are the Marashea. It might be them.'

'The who?' asked Garrett.

'The Marashea,' answered Petrus. 'They're Basothos from Lesotho. They call themselves Marashea, which is a bastardisation of the word Russians or Ama-Russian. Lesotho is a shit place. Full of mountains. They're all mad. Fight all the time, treat women like shit.'

'Oh, and Zulu's don't fight?' quipped Garrett.

'That's different,' argued Petrus. 'We fight for a reason. These little buggers have an expression; they say, "We are fighting the world." And they believe it. You don't want to cross them. It's like the whole country belongs to one huge street gang. You insult one and you insult all. The rest of us tend to leave them alone if we can.'

'You think that it could be them?'

'I hope not,' said Petrus. 'Would make life really difficult for us. I know one of their elders. Guy called Ramajato. I reckon that we go visit him; it's as good a place as any to start. We'll see what he has to say.' The Zulu stood up. 'Thanks, Jovito.'

The young gangster smiled. 'Always and anytime, *baba*.'

Chief superintendent Hung Gwok of the Hong Kong Customs and Excise was trying his best not to appear intimidated. And afraid.

Tai Zeng sat at his desk and stared at the customs officer. Tai's face was blank. There was no hint of the anger that roiled within him. To show emotion in front of a weasel like Gwok would be improper and would ultimately involve loss of face or *mian zi*.

'Thirteen horns, chief superintendent,' said Tai. 'Almost four million dollars American.'

'But, Chiang Tai,' interjected Gwok, using the honorific, chiang to show his respect. 'You must understand my position. As the chief superintendent I am responsible for the search and seizure of all contraband that comes through Hong Kong harbors and airports. If I do not show occasional results then those higher up will become suspicious.'

'Yes, superintendent,' said Tai. 'I agree. But four million dollars? If you needed a show of efficiency you should have spoken to me and I would have supplied a shipment of a single horn, three hundred thousand dollars or so. There was no need to steal four million dollars from me.'

'Once again, chiang Tai,' answered Gwok. 'I offer my most sincere apologies. But I must add, kàn qíngkuàng, please see things from my point of view. The risks that I take are exceptionally high. The penalty for what I do is death. Perhaps, and, once again chiang Tai, I impart the greatest respect upon you, but perhaps, if my remuneration was to be increased then there would be less chance of things like this happening again.'

Tai Zeng was absolutely incredulous. So much so that, for a shameful few seconds, he lost his control and, with it, his mian zi.

'Are you threatening me?' he questioned. 'Are you attempting to horse trade with me? You fucking mainland peasant, how dare you?'

Gwok smirked at both Tai Zeng's loss of control and of face. For the first time in his dealings with the triad enforcer, he felt he had the upper hand. He was in a position of power and both of them knew it.

'How dare I? I am a chief inspector. If I were in the army, I would command the rank of senior colonel. And what are you? A drug smuggler and a dealer in fake medicines and fables. No, Tai Zeng, I say, how dare you? From this month onwards my stipend will be raised by five hundred percent. If not, then I foresee that many more shipments of horn will be discovered and confiscated.' The superintendent stood up. 'Our meeting is over. I trust that you have seen my point of view and agree.' Gwok bowed. 'Now, I bid you goodbye.' He left the room.

Tai watched the customs officer leave.

For a long while the enforcer did not react. He sat still. Silent.

Finally, he leant forward and pressed his intercom.

'Mingyu, contact mister Hubert. Set up a meeting at his earliest convenience. I will see him here, at the office. Afterwards, come through to my office.'

He sat back in his seat. His anger at Gwok roiled in his gut but he controlled it. Mister Hubert would sort the problem out.

And as for his anger…for that there was Mingyu.

CHAPTER FIFTEEN

Different sort, those youngsters,' said Garrett.

'And then some,' agreed Petrus. 'The strange thing is that some of them are from privileged backgrounds. Middle class parents. Good schools. Now their lives are all about whether to wear Pierre Cardin or Rocco Borroco. Whether to steal an Audi or a BMW. And I tell you something; those choices can be life or death decisions. They have a code that they call, Uwiles. Basically, that means, to fall out of fashion. Someone who wears the wrong labels or drives the wrong car, the unfashionable choice, is considered Uwiles. And that means that he obviously can't afford the latest and the best. He is no longer at the top of his game. If that happens, it isn't long before someone challenges you, or simply shoots you in the back.'

'Tough life.'

'Maybe,' admitted Petrus. 'But they're nothing compared to the new breed of gangster that'll hit the streets soon.

'Who?'

'AIDS orphans,' answered Petrus. 'Over quarter of a million of them. No parents, no hope, no life. How much respect for life do you reckon those dudes will have when they are all living under a death penalty? I'll tell you - fuck all.'

'But AIDS isn't necessarily a death penalty anymore,' argued Garrett.

'It is in Africa, man,' countered Petrus. 'Haven't got no NHS here. You get sick, you pay or you die. Simple.'

They drove for another twenty minutes in silence. Garrett pondered a life without hope or reprieve. Then he stopped. It was depressing and he had enough to worry about without creating even more stress for himself.

At one stage, Petrus pulled over and went into a shop. He came out with a large bag and put it onto the back seat.

'We're almost there,' he said as he got back into the vehicle. 'Weleda Township. Now, bear in mind that these Basothos are full of shit. But the guy that we're going to see, Ramajato, can be an extra touchy fucker, so be respectful. I'll call him Ramo, but you call him mister Ramajato or Doctor.'

'Why?' Asked Garrett. 'Is he a doctor?'

'Not sure. Probably not, but if it's doctor he wants, it's doctor he gets, okay?'

Garrett nodded.

Petrus took a couple of wrong turns and had to backtrack, eventually, he found the house that he was looking for. The dwellings were modest, one or two rooms each. Ramajato's was no larger than any of the others. But, unlike the township they had just been in, this was spotless. The streets were swept clean. The dwellings were painted in vibrant colors. Reds, oranges, purples. The dogs were well fed as opposed to looking like mobile toast racks. Washing was hung up in plain view with no worry of theft. There was an aura of, if not prosperity, then at least stability.

'Not a bad area,' commented Garrett.

'Yep,' agreed the Zulu. 'These Marashea police themselves. You step out of line, then a bunch of guys come visiting and re-educate you using big sticks and sharp implements.'

'Tough love,' quipped Garrett.

'Don't know about love. But definitely tough.'

Petrus grabbed the packet he had purchased as they got out of the pick up and went to the front door.

Petrus knocked.

The door was opened by a tiny woman. She was dressed in a floral frock over which she had draped a blanket of many colors. It was clasped at her throat with an intricate copper brooch.

'I have come to see, Ramajato,' said Petrus.

She bowed and clapped her hands. They followed her into the house.

The door led directly into a living, cooking area. There was a wood-burning stove. A large freestanding tin basin. A single cold-water tap. A cheap, well-scrubbed, table with six matching steel-legged chairs.

At one of the chairs sat an old man. Long gray beard. A crop of white hair. Huge brass hoop earrings in each ear.

He was smoking one of the largest pipes that Garrett had ever seen. A stupendous affair that looked like a beer stein on the end of a length of industrial pipe.

His eyes lit up with pleasure when he saw Petrus.

'Hey,' he greeted. 'It's the baboon. What are you doing here? Come for advice from your betters?'

Petrus grinned. 'Better a baboon than a little old monkey that sits in the trees and chatters at its superiors.'

'Enough pleasantries,' said the old man. 'Did you bring me any tobacco?'

Petrus handed him the bag. He opened it and took out a large sack of Navy cut tobacco. Rough and strong.

He nodded and then looked at Garrett.

'I need lots of tobacco,' he said. 'This pipe needs plenty of fuel. So,' he continued. 'I am Ramajato, who are you?'

'Greetings, doctor,' said the soldier. 'I am Petrus' friend, Garrett.'

The old man nodded. 'The possessed one.'

Garrett raised an eyebrow. 'Apparently so.'

'What do I owe this visit to, Petrus?'

The Zulu told him, starting with Malusi's murder, the Rhino poaching and ending with their visit to the amagents.

'Okay, so how can we help you?' asked the Doctor.

'Well, first we had to check that the Russian wasn't aMarashea. I know you so I thought that it would make sense to come here first.'

'What would we want with rhino horn? There is no magik in it.'

'You can sell it for a great deal of money,' interjected Garrett.

'Really?' asked Ramajato, his voice redolent with disbelief.

Garrett nodded. 'Eighty thousand dollars a kilogram. That's almost a million Rands.'

The old man stared at Garrett for a few seconds and then he burst out laughing. 'For a horn. I got some goat horns; you want to give me a million for those?'

'Only rhino horn,' said Garrett.

Ramajato laughed again and shook his head. 'Why? Horn is horn. It doesn't do anything. It's just like fingernails. Or hair.'

'I know,' agreed Garrett.

'But still, you will pay a million for it?'

'Not me,' corrected Garrett. 'Other people. The Russian.'

Abruptly Petrus stood up. 'We need to go, old friend,' he said.

Ramajato nodded. 'Yes. You have work to do. I am sorry that I cannot help. But you can be certain that it not us.'

He showed them to the door. Outside they were approached by another Basotho who was coming to visit Ramajato.

The old man introduced them. 'Banjo, this is Petrus. This is his friend, Garrett. He is a funny man. He says that he can sell the horn of the *Ditshukudu* for one million Rands.'

Banjo burst out laughing. 'Well then,' he said. 'I have a bargain for you.' He thrust his hips forward. 'You can have a slice of my horn for half that. It's so big I really won't miss a piece.'

The two Basotho's doubled over with mirth.

Petrus grinned.

Garrett simply looked baffled; the local sense of humor evaded him.

The two friends climbed into their vehicle and drove off.

'Well, it's not them,' said Petrus. 'They didn't even know that there's a market for rhino horn.'

'Yep,' agreed Garrett. 'And anyone with a sense of humor that is so basic doesn't have the brains to run a crime syndicate.'

Petrus smiled. 'Don't take offence. They weren't laughing at you. They were just laughing because they felt like laughing. They pretty much would have laughed at anything. You were simply the easiest available target.'

Garrett said nothing.

After a few minutes Petrus slipped his cell into the hands-free and dialed a number.

Jovito answered. 'Hey, Petrus.'

'Hey, Jovito. Just finished with the Marashea's. It's a bust. Not them.'

'Sorry to hear that.'

'I'm not,' said Petrus. 'Rather take on the whole Russian army that those cantankerous little bastards. So, what next?'

'Best bet would be Yuri Olokoff - owns a few clubs in and around Hillbrow. He specializes in kidnappings, mostly kids. Picks them up outside schools and such and then sells them back to their parents. If they don't pay up straight away, he sends them a body part, ears, fingers, that sort of thing. He keeps the ransoms fairly low and pays off enough cops so that the whole operation stays pretty low key. He also traffics in stolen cars and protection, drugs, IDB. Bad man. Lives in Parktown North. Here, I got his address.'

Jovito read out an address.

'Thanks, man,' acknowledged Petrus. 'We'll check the place out.'

'Be safe,' said Jovito.

Petrus cut the connection. 'So,' he said. 'You heard that?'

Garrett scowled. 'Don't like people who kidnap kids.'

Petrus nodded. 'I think we go and talk to this man. Explain the error of his ways to him. Hopefully he's also the one that we are looking for.'

Hung Gwok's position as chief superintendent rated him a car but not a driver. Drivers were only supplied to those with a rank of Assistant Commissioner or higher.

His official salary of 7800 US Dollars a month allowed him to rent a small single room apartment in the Sheung Wan area of the main island. Comfortable but in no way luxurious. Hung Gwok, however, did not live in a single bedroom apartment in Sheug Wan. He lived in a three-bedroom, sea view apartment in the popular Robinson Road. This was due to the fact that Tai Lung provided a top up to his official salary that was more than generous.

But Hung was ambitious. He wanted more. Much more.

Unfortunately, he was a man whose ambition was coupled with very little else. He was not overly bright; he was boring in both thought and deed and he had an over inflated view of his own worth.

However, what he lacked in raw intelligence he made up for in paranoia.

He glanced in the rear-view mirror of his new, canary yellow, VW Golf convertible and noticed a white Toyota SUV. He was convinced that it was the same vehicle that had pulled out behind him when he had left work. To check if he was being followed, he took a series of random, lefts and rights.

The SUV stayed with him.

The customs official began to sweat.

Perhaps he had overstepped the boundaries with Tai Zeng. Maybe he should have been happy with what he already had. Content with triple his actual wage.

With fear- fumbling fingers he leant over, opened his glove compartment and pulled out a Norinco CF-98 pistol.

The Chinese pistol had a slight patina of rust on it, partly due to the humid coastal air and partly because of the complete lack of care and maintenance time spent on it. Shoddy. Like its owner's thought process.

With the comforting weight of steel in his lap, Gwok drove randomly around Hong Kong. Reversing, doing U-turns and nipping down short one-way streets until he could no longer see the white Toyota anymore.

Satisfied, he drove directly home.

Gwok pulled into his underground parking, got out of his car and slipped the pistol into his belt in the small of his back.

He then took the elevator to his apartment, unlocked the door and went inside.

A feeling of relief washed over him and then he chuckled to himself.

'Stupid,' he said to himself. 'Don't let paranoia get the better of you.'

'But sometimes a little paranoia can be a healthy thing, mister Gwok,' said a voice from the shadows.

Gwok spun around, his stomach cramping with fear.

A man stepped forward, out of the darkness.

He was small. Caucasian. Gray hair cut short back and sides. A toothbrush moustache. Dark, off the rack suit. Polished, well worn, black leather shoes. Round spectacles. Bad teeth.

In his hand he held a Ruger 22 pistol with a Checkmate suppressor screwed onto the end of the barrel.

Gwok contemplated going for his weapon but the man shook his head.

'No, no, Hung, you don't mind if I call you Hung? Considering how close we are about to become I feel that it is appropriate to be on first name terms.'

'I don't know your first name.'

'Of course you don't. My apologies. I am, mister Hubert, or simply, Hubert if you prefer. Now, take the pistol out of your belt and drop it on the floor. Use two fingers only. Kick it over to me. Oaky, turn around, hands behind your back.'

Gwok complied. He felt cold steel against his wrists. Then he heard the click of handcuffs.

'Very good. Please, sit down.'

'Would it do any good if I recanted my demands?' Asked Gwok, his voice shaking with fear.

Hubert shrugged. 'I have no idea what your demands were, Hung. Nor do I care.'

'So. There is no leeway. I attempt to negotiate and so I die.'

'Yes, it seems that way,' agreed Hubert. 'But mister Zeng did have a message. He said to tell you - "Place your hand in a bucket full of water. After a while remove it. The hole that you have left in the water is the exact amount of worth that he places on you".'

Hung closed his eyes. Tears ran from them. Hot and slow. Fear. Remorse. Self-pity.

He took a deep. 'Okay, do it.'

Hubert smiled. An expression close to pity on his face. A doctor informing a patient of a terminal disease.

'Oh, I am sorry, Hung, but there shall be no quick exit for you. Unfortunately, mister Zeng has asked me to make an example of you.'

Hubert stepped forward, pulled a roll of duct tape from his pocket and expertly stuck a patch over Hung's mouth. Then he wound the rest of the roll around Hung, strapping him securely to the chair.

Finally, he stood back and raised his pistol.

The Ruger coughed asthmatically. Twice.

Hung shuddered, unable to either move or scream. Blood poured from his shattered kneecaps, soaking the legs of his trousers and filling his shoes.

Hubert stood over the customs officer and stroked his forehead.

'Quiet now,' he urged. 'Take the pain. Embrace it. Attempting to thrash about like that will only make it worse.'

Hubert waited patiently for Hung to settle down.

And then there was the sound of a blade being flicked open. And the light reflected off the edge of the straight razor. A sliver of silver sharpness in the dark.

'Now, Hung,' said Hubert. His voice quiet. Reassuring. Almost friendly. 'I am going to start by cutting off your eyelids.'

Yuri Olokoff's residence in Parktown North was a massive double story pile. Fifteen-foot-high walls with another three feet of electric fencing on the top. Guard dogs, remote controlled gates. A guardhouse and floodlights.

'Problem,' said Garrett. 'Can't see in so we got no real idea how many guards there are. Floodlights everywhere. Even if we manage to evade the electric fence there's the dogs. Not sure what to do.'

Petrus sat for a while, deep in thought. 'I've got an idea,' he said. 'Let's take a drive around the block.'

After a couple of turns he pointed at a small beige painted structure on the side of the road. 'There. Stop the car.'

Garrett pulled over.

Petrus got out, walked down the street for a few yards and then disappeared into someone's house, via their open gate.

He reappeared less than a minute later, a length of green hosepipe in his one hand and a plastic watering can in the other.

'Just doing a bit of alternative shopping,' he informed Garrett.

'You mean, stealing.'

Petrus shrugged. 'Whatever.'

He unscrewed the gas cap, slid the hose in and then proceeded to siphon off a can full of gas. When the watering can was full, he screwed the gas tank cover back on.

'What now?' enquired Garrett who had, up until this point, watched the whole process without question.

Petrus pointed, once again, at the small beige structure. 'Electrical substation,' he said.

Then he walked over and sprinkled the entire can of gas over the substation. Finally, he stood back, lit a cigarette, took a drag and then threw the rest at the gasoline-soaked substation.

The structure went up with a sound akin to a giant dog barking. A deep woof and a spectacular ball of flame.

'I suggest that we bugger off for a while,' said Petrus. 'Won't be long and the electricity to the area will blow. The electrical department are so useless that it'll be days before they fix it. Yuri will have backup generators, everybody does, but I reckon they'll only drive the necessities, electric fence, gate, some lights. The main floodlights should go out, so that will help.'

'But the electric fence alarm will go off when we breach it,' said Garrett.

'Do not fear, I have a cunning plan,' replied Petrus. 'What we do first, we break down one of the branches that are hanging over the electric fence, drop it on and set off the alarm. When they come check it out, we wait. Then after an hour or so, we do it again. I guarantee that they take their time getting there the second time, so we can scale the fence and get inside. Now, I'm not sure how many people they have but it looks like one on the gate. I'd guess that there are probably three more in the grounds, one or two inside plus Yuri. So, seven, maybe ten. We better go in fully armed Blades, 45 and AK's. What do you think?'

'A lot of ifs and buts and shoulds,' quipped Garrett. 'But I got nothing, so any plan is better than no plan at all.'

The first part of Petrus' plan went well. The electricity blew, they dropped a branch on the fencing, repeated the act an hour later and, true to Petrus' assumptions, they managed to get into the grounds without being detected.

The two of them lay under a copse of ornamental bushes and scanned their surrounds. Petrus' estimation of the quantity of guards that Yuri would have was off. Way off.

He had figured on seven. Maybe ten, tops.

From their vantage point Garrett could see at least twelve men and five dogs. Inside the house many of the lights were on and he could see the silhouettes of men as they walked past the undraped windows. Maybe another six or seven. Not counting Yuri himself.

So, closer to twenty. Double their worst estimate.

'Not a problem,' whispered Petrus. 'We go in, real quiet. Find Yuri, question him, do the necessary and get out.'

'Okay,' agreed Garrett as he checked the magazines on his AK. He had taped two together, back-to-back. Petrus only had one mag. Garrett had his Colt copy as backup.

The two of them moved towards the house. In the night they were in their element. Mere shadows amongst the darkness, they slipped from cover to cover until they were at a large open window.

Garrett checked for alarms and tripwires, saw nothing and rolled in over the windowsill. Petrus followed.

All hell broke loose.

An ear-piercing alarm went off and the sound of shouting and running feet joined in the cacophony.

'What the fuck?' shouted Petrus. 'I thought that you checked.'

'I did,' argued Garrett. 'Must be some sort of infrared beam or motion detector. I couldn't see anything.'

The soldier glanced around them. They appeared to be in some sort of gymnasium. Chromed machines lined the wall, blue exercise mats on the floor. Along the one corner stood a brick-built wet bar, complete with fresh juice dispensers and a glass fronted refrigerator stocked with a variety of energy drinks.

'We need a new plan,' shouted Petrus. 'Guards coming. Plenty of them.' He pointed through the window at a group of seven or eight guards with a pack of dogs running towards them.

Garrett paused for a second as he crunched through all of the avenues open to them.

'Garrett,' yelled Petrus. 'Getting urgent here.'

'Shit,' shouted Garrett. 'I got nothing.'

'How about we shoot them?' asked Petrus.

'Might as well,' answered Garrett. 'Can't think of anything else.'

Petrus lined up his AK and pulled the trigger on full automatic, emptying the entire magazine in two and a half seconds. One of the attackers and two dogs went down. Petrus ducked.

'I'm out of ammo.'

'That was quick,' said Garrett as he checked that his fire-selector was on single shot. He leant against the windowsill and fired, sweeping from left to right. Each shot aimed. Each shot counting.

The last dog almost made it to the window. None of the men came even close.

Another three guards came running into view but before Garrett could shoot, they lay down a torrent of fire. Steel jacketed slugs buzzed and whined around the room and the window simply disintegrated.

'More coming down the corridor,' shouted Petrus.

'Behind the bar,' said Garrett.

The two of them sprinted across the room and jumped behind the brick-built bar.

Just in time.

The door burst open and another group of men opened fire. MP5's, AK's and pistols.

Garrett popped his AK over the top of the bar and pulled the trigger until it ran dry. Then he changed the magazine and fired again.

After under a minute he was out so he drew his Colt.

Petrus had drawn his assegai.

'We are in deep shit,' said Garrett.

'You don't say?' quipped Petrus sarcastically.

Garrett leant around the bar and fired off a few rounds. The resultant return fire was deafening.

'Come on, *Isosha*,' urged Petrus. 'Make a plan. Quickly.'

'If this was an alcoholic bar, maybe,' said Garrett. 'We could chuck some vodka at them and then light it up.'

The soldier handed the Colt to Petrus and started to frantically root through the contents of the cupboards, looking for anything that might help them.

Petrus popped off the occasional round to keep the guards from rushing them.

'Ha,' exclaimed Garrett. He pulled a twenty-liter gas container out of one of the cupboards. 'Liquid nitrogen,' he said. 'They use it to make fruit juice slushies.' He turned to Petrus. 'Give me the Colt.'

The Zulu complied.

'Right,' continued Garrett. 'Now, chuck this gas container over the bar. Make sure it gets high. Above head height.'

'Then what?' asked Petrus.

'Then duck, my friend.'

Petrus hefted the container in his two hands. 'Okay,' he said. 'On three. One, two,' he tossed the canister over the bar and into the air.

Garrett popped up like a meerkat with a semi-automatic pistol.

Aimed.

Fired.

The room simply exploded.

The door disappeared down the corridor, the ceiling lifted and then fell into the room, all of the plaster fell off the walls and one of the walls blew out, leaving a gaping hole into the sitting room next to it.

Garrett stood up, Colt in hand, and glanced around the room. Petrus was sitting on the floor, legs splayed out in front of him like a child at play. Blood poured down his face from a jagged cut across his forehead.

Bodies lay scattered about the room. Broken and twisted. Dolls tossed aside in a child's tantrum.

Blood decorated the walls and what was left of the ceiling. There were some body parts no longer attached to their relevant bodies. An arm. A couple of fingers. A shoe, complete with foot.

There was a dull throb in Garrett's left shoulder. He glanced down at it. A small, jagged piece of metal had lodged itself in his shoulder pad. He grabbed it and pulled. It came loose with an audible sucking sound and a lance of pain shot through him.

Petrus struggled to his feet, weeping the blood from his eyes with the back of his hand.

'What the hell,' he mumbled. 'How did that happen?'

'When liquid nitrogen vaporizes, it expands by a factor of over seven hundred,' said Garrett. That's as close as damn it to TNT. Must admit, though, I didn't expect such a huge explosion.'

Someone groaned, over by the door, obviously he had arrived last. Garrett walked over.

The man lay on the floor, partially covered with ceiling board. Garrett pulled off the debris and knelt down beside him.

He was badly wounded. A shard of metal had creased across his stomach and opened it up like a zipper. He was desperately attempting to hold his guts in with his hands. Breathing in short gasps, his face white with both shock and pain.

'Help me.'

'Maybe,' said Garrett. 'It all depends on you. What's your name?'

'Yuri,' the man gasped. 'Yuri Olokoff.'

'Hey,' exclaimed Petrus. 'Stroke of luck there. Things are looking up.'

'Tell me, Yuri,' said Garrett. 'Do you deal in rhino horn?'

'I'm dying,' grunted the Russian.'

'Maybe,' agreed Garrett. 'Definitely will unless you get some sort of medical attention.'

'Help me.'

'First, Yuri, answer my question. Do you deal in rhino horn?'

The wounded Russian looked at Garrett with an expression of incredulity on his face.

'I'm fucking dying here,' he said. 'My guts are falling out. I need a hospital. Who are you? What are you doing here? Get me some fucking help.'

'It's a simple question, Yuri,' continued Garrett. 'Answer it and we'll see what we can do.'

'Fuck you', gasped Yuri. 'I'm not saying anything until you call an ambulance.'

Petrus strode over and kicked the Russian in the side. He screamed in pain.

'Talk, you useless fuck,' shouted Petrus. 'Talk or I will kick the rest of your guts out onto the floor. I'm looking for the person that murdered my baby brother. I don't give a shit about you or your problems, you drug dealing, child kidnapping shit. Talk now or I will strangle you with your own intestines.'

'Okay,' grunted Yuri. 'I got nothing to do with rhino horn. I deal in drugs, girls, a bit of illicit diamond buying, protection, that sort of thing.'

'And child kidnapping,' added Garrett.

'Yes, okay. Some kidnapping. But no rhinos,' insisted Yuri. 'And anyway, I never killed any of the kids, simply removed a few body parts. Collateral damage of a sort. Fuck sakes. You could have just phoned me and asked. No reason to kill everyone and blow my guts out. You guys are mental cases.'

'Yeah, sorry,' said Garrett. 'Things got a little out of hand. Still, karma, hey?'

'Karma what?' asked Yuri.

'Live by the sword, die by the sword. That sort of karma.'

'No, wait,' said Yuri. 'Don't leave me. I can help. I think that the guy that you're looking for is Hubenko. Viktor Hubenko. He's not Russian, he's Ukrainian. Works with a guy called Tai something. Chinese. If someone killed your brother then it probably got something to do with Viktor and his guys. He's a complete fucking lunatic, six foot eight, bull of a man. Shaved head and eyebrows. Has a group of three ex-alpha group Ukraine Special Forces. Yarik, Igor and Stas.'

'Where do we find him?' enquired Petrus.

'He lives in Honeydew, a smallholding. Called "High Chaparral" like that television show, "Bonanza".'

'The house in Bonanza was called Ponderosa,' corrected Garrett.

'Yeah, that. Ponder-something,' agreed Yuri. 'Now get me to hospital,' he screamed. 'I don't deserve to be left like this.'

'Yeah, tell that to the kids whose ears you cut off,' said Garrett as he stood up and followed Petrus from the room.

'I'll drive,' said the Zulu. 'We need to check out this Viktor guy's place. Plan our next move.'

'I agree,' said Garrett. 'But first we need to stitch that cut in your head. It doesn't look good.'

They left via the window, scaled the fence, got into the Land Cruiser and drove off.

Eventually Yuri stopped screaming.

CHAPTER EIGHTEEN

Colonel Chang believed in delegation of responsibility.

Most protection rackets are run by a group of criminals who send their muscle out to canvas businesses in their area of influence and convince them that paying a monthly stipend to the group would result in their business not being burned down, or robbed. Or the owner suffering from some form of grievous bodily harm.

Chang had ratcheted the business model up a notch and, instead of working at the street level, he sent master sergeant Lu Feng, along with a contingent of heavily armed Flying Tiger Special Forces, to visit the local heads of the various crime families.

It was sergeant Feng's job to educate the gangsters regarding the colonel's new system. The new business model went - Pay us fifty percent of all your takings, or else thirty-two well-armed elite troops will make sure that you, your family, your friends and everybody that they knew, will end up either dead or wishing that they were dead.

Although the model had met with some initial resistance, a few very gory and very public deaths had convinced all of its merit.

As a result, colonel Jin Chang was well on his way to becoming a relatively wealthy man.

He sat in his study, on a buffalo-covered wingback chair, behind a hand carved teak desk. The rest of the room was decorated in a masculine blend of Africa and China. Chunky hardwood table and chairs, painted silk pictures, a lacquered black liquor cabinet. An ice-maker.

The study, situated in a mansion in Borrowdale, Zimbabwe, had nothing to do with his military rank or profession. In fact, it was strictly illegal for any officer of the People's Army to live off their appointed military base.

But in a country where true power is still obtained through the barrel of a gun, Jin Chang was the law. There were some higher-ranking officers in Harare and surrounds, but there were none who were superior to him. He was the Yi Deng Bo or chief of the first rank.

A ruler of his own fiefdom.

The fact that he was making a fortune was immaterial - money was a mere way of keeping the score. He liked living in Africa. He liked having his own private army. He liked being a king. China held no draw for him.

He knew that, at some stage, the Peoples Government would recall him. But that was a bridge to be crossed when it came into view.

He did know one thing for sure, there was no way that he would ever return to China.

He would defect. He had enough money to lose himself anywhere in the world. From Africa to America to Asia. There was no way that he would ever again set foot in the huge stinking, corrupt cesspool that was Red China again - he would rather do all that he could to stay in the huge stinking, corrupt cesspool that was Africa.

Today was the first Wednesday of the month. As a result, there was a queue of people outside. Normal people. Mainly black. Some white. Some Asian. All waiting patiently.

Predominantly they had come for favor. A few would have come for advice. Maybe one or two with offerings of some sort. But mainly they would be asking for favor. Help with a business dispute. A delay in protection monies paid. His presence at a son's wedding.

Some up and coming gang lords would ask if they could buy weapons. And he would oblige. Antiquated AK's, suspect explosives, corroded ammunition. Then he would explain how the system of tribute worked. And his empire would expand a little bit more.

And he would see them all. Because he was Yi Deng Bo and these were his subjects. He feared no one.

Except, of course, Tai Zeng and the triads. Anyone in their right mind feared them. They were beyond ruthless and they did not suffer double crossers or traitors. Not that this bothered the colonel; after all, most of his income came from the rhino horn and ivory that he supplied Tai Zeng, so he had no intention of biting the hand that fed him - especially if that hand could bite back.

Sergeant Lu Feng opened the door and ushered the next supplicant in. An old man, suit worn shiny with age, hat in hand.

Colonel Chang smiled.

He liked to put his subjects at ease.

CHAPTER NINETEEN

T hese things don't work,' said Garrett as he peered through the large pair of binoculars.

'Yes, they do,' said Petrus. 'They're just old. I think that there's a crack in the prism.'

'I can see two of everything.'

'Close one eye then,' advised the Zulu.

'That's better. Fine if you're a cyclops,' responded Garrett as he swung his vision across the house in front of them. 'Jesus, this place is crawling with protection. Teams of guards, floodlights, electric fencing. There're no dogs. Why? I don't like it when there aren't any dogs.'

'I do, says Petrus. Don't like killing dogs. Makes me feel bad. They're only doing what they're told.'

Garrett continued to scan the area, laying out quadrants in his mind and then meticulously scanning them. Eventually he spoke.

'I see, that's why.' He passed the monocular binoculars to Petrus. 'Take a look. Three o'clock from the main building. Between the main building and that one guardhouse.'

Petrus adjusted the focus and looked. 'I see it,' he confirmed. 'A tripwire.'

'Yep,' agreed Garrett. 'Follow it.'

Petrus ran his gaze along the steel wire. 'A green box. Is it a mine?'

'Yep,' said Garrett. 'Claymores. If you keep looking you can pick up more of them. They're everywhere. We're lucky, the angle of the sun picks up the wire. Another ten minutes and the angle will be too low. They'll be invisible again. But that's why they don't have dogs roaming around. They would set off the mines.'

'Scary,' admitted Petrus.

'Very,' confirmed Garrett. 'So, we've got a hard perimeter, claymores everywhere, four guard houses, probably with machine guns, two guards in each hut. Two more couples patrolling the perimeter. I'm sure that there's a whole bunch more inside.'

'But no dogs,' said Petrus.

'No dogs,' agreed Garrett.

'Suggestions?'

Garrett shrugged. 'Go somewhere else. Somewhere far away. This place is a fortress. There's no way that we can get in here without being seen, and even if we did there's too many of them for us to overcome. It's a lose, lose situation. Maybe if we had amour, artillery and air support, but otherwise I'm fresh out of ideas - sorry.'

Petrus pulled a stick of biltong, South African dried beef, out of his pocket. He bit off a piece and lay on the ground, chewing thoughtfully.

Eventually he spoke. 'What if I could get us some armor and artillery. Could we do it then?'

'Is this a serious question?' asked Garrett.

'Deadly.'

'Well then we might stand a chance. Not alone though. We would need some help. Can you do it?'

Petrus nodded in the affirmative, although he didn't look that confident. 'I think so,' he answered. 'But it'll cost.'

Ngyen Van was one of the richest men in Hanoi, Vietnam. He had made his money by buying huge tracts of land in the 1990's that was now worth over one thousand times more. He had made hundreds of millions of dollars profit and he was determined that everybody knew it.

Firstly, he had purchased a collection of fifty super-cars and then an empty lot in the middle of Hanoi on which he parked his cars, together with a serious amount of protection. Then he took over two hundred poster sized photos of himself surrounded by various trappings of his wealth and placed them, in frames, around the cars. Finally, he had a life size wax model of himself placed on a throne in the middle of the lot, under a cover. Then he opened the lot for public viewing.

The strangest thing about his incredibly megalomaniacal project was the fact that he had actually copied it from a wealthy entrepreneur who lived in Ho Chi Minh City. Lifestyles of the rich and tasteless.

But impressing the local peons was a relatively easy task. Impressing fellow multi-millionaires, however, took a little more thought.

So, Ngyen Van threw a party.

He greeted his guests wearing his gold and platinum sunglasses and custom diamond encrusted Rolex ushering them into the main banquet hall that featured Salangane's nests and caviar. Food purchased for over ten thousand dollars a pound in a country where the average wage was less than one hundred dollars per month.

A perfect example of the utter failure of a one-party communist state and its ability to ensure that workers enjoyed the same levels of luxury as the ruling classes.

But even this was not enough. So, the Vietnamese oligarch organized a shipment of something that was more expensive than cocaine. More expensive than gold.

He had obtained two hundred grams of powdered Rhino horn.

This was combined with a variety of cocktails to create the ultimate billionaire's alcoholic drink, instantly changing the alcohol of your choice from a ten-dollar drink into a two-thousand-dollar drink.

The ultimate in conspicuous consumption.

The rhino horn did the trick and the party was a huge success.

CHAPTER TWENTY-ONE

We call her, Aunty Beulah,' said Petrus, talking as he drove. 'Aunty was the leader of a large SPU. A Self Protection Unit, back in the days of the struggle. While we were all busy fighting apartheid, the two main black parties, the ANC and the Zulu Inkatha Freedom Party, were also jostling for power. We both wanted to assure our power bases before the first elections came along. Man, it was bloody. I reckon maybe twenty thousand people got killed in that struggle alone, not counting the war against apartheid. And I tell you,' continued Petrus. 'Aunty was responsible for a significant percentage of those deaths.'

The Zulu shifted in his seat and tried to locate his pack of cigarettes. Eventually he gave up.

'Got any smokes?'

Garrett nodded.

'Well light up then.'

Garrett knocked out two cigarettes, lit. Passed one over.

'Thanks,' said Petrus. 'Now, after Mandela had been released and the political situation had levelled out,

Aunty Beulah went into semi-retirement and moved to a farm outside of Ladysmith in Natal. Many of her former SPU soldiers and their families had stayed on with her and she ran her farm as a collective. Not communist, you know. More like an Israeli kibbutz. Each person or family received compensation dependent on their needs, regardless of what position that they held.'

The Zulu pinched the butt of his cigarette, killing the fire. Then he flicked it out of the window onto the tarmacadam road. 'Obviously Aunty Beulah deemed her needs to be significantly larger than everybody else's. But no one minded, I mean, she was the leader and they also respected her as a great warrior.'

'So not really like a kibbutz then,' quipped Garrett. 'More like a fiefdom.'

Petrus thought for a while. 'Maybe,' he admitted. 'Anyway, after she retired, she kept a large arsenal ranging from AK47's, R1's, various sidearms, a selection of grenades and anti-personal mines, two 7.62mm light machine guns, a 12.7mm Browning heavy machine gun and two 60mm commando mortar systems with hundreds of rounds of high explosive ammunition. She was also rumored to have a Casspir armored vehicle and a heavy 120mm mortar. So, she's the one that we need.'

'If she still has all of that stuff,' qualified Garrett.

'If she does,' agreed Petrus.

The Zulu turned off the main road onto a single lane B-road. After half an hour he turned off that onto a dirt road that eventually became a simple dirt track. Finally, he turned off the track onto what could only be described as a trail.

The Land Cruiser bumped slowly along the trail in low ratio four-wheel drive. The car was air-conditioned but both Garrett and Petrus preferred their air to be real, so the windows were wound down, allowing the dry hot air to circulate. It didn't do much to dissipate the appalling heat. In fact it simply seemed to turn the cab into a fan oven. Solar powered. Environmentally friendly.

'We're being watched,' said Garrett.

Petrus nodded. 'I know, seen two youngsters with cell phones. Hiding in the bush.'

'I've seen three,' countered Garrett.

'It's not a competition,' said Petrus.

'Of course it is,' argued the soldier.

Petrus laughed. 'True.'

Eventually, they arrived at a fence. Barbed wire, rusted but taut. There was a gate. It was padlocked.

A young boy appeared out of the long grass, unlocked the large brass padlock and opened the gate for them. They drove through and it was locked behind them.

Fifteen minutes of kidney bruising driving and they came to the main farm. The houses were set out in a semi-traditional way. A circle of dwellings with what was obviously Aunty Beulah's house, top and center, and then progressively smaller ones to each side.

However, there was no central kraal for the cattle, they were penned in fenced areas to the sides of the dwellings in a more western style arrangement.

Some of the dwellings had satellite television discs on their roofs. The larger houses also had pick-ups or battered SUV's parked in front of them.

There were two armed guards standing outside Aunty Beulah's house. Both carried AK's. The weapons were clean. As were the guard's khaki quasi-military uniforms. Pressed and in good order. Boots and belts well-polished. Only their berets spoiled the effect, pushed back on their heads instead of placed on the head with the edge binding one inch above eyebrows and straight across forehead.

They waved Petrus to a parking space at the side of the house.

Petrus parked and he and Garrett got out.

The guards showed them through the front door and closed it behind them.

The door opened straight into the sitting room. Aunty Beulah was sitting on a large, mustard green, chintz covered chair, the arms worn shiny with age. The rest of the furniture was an eclectic mix. Two corduroy sofas, a leather wingback and a new chrome and black leather Italian-looking recliner. There was also a hoard of various coffee tables scattered about the room, seemingly at random.

On one particular table, in front of Aunty, was a tray with a teapot, three mugs, sugar, a tin of sweetened condensed milk and buttermilk rusks.

Aunty stood to greet them; her hand outstretched. She was a tall woman. Taller than both Garrett and Petrus. Six four at least. And big. Not fat, simply large. Raw boned and sturdy.

She wore a purple kaftan that complimented her lashings of purple eye makeup. On her cheeks, two vivid spots of red blusher. Like a huge, demented clown.

Atop her head, the most extraordinary wig that Garrett had ever seen. An Afro made from hyper-glossy manmade fiber. And she wore it like a fur hat, with not even the vaguest nod towards realism or fashion. It sat on top of her head like her guards' berets. Two sizes too small and precariously perched. A comic figure.

Until you looked into her eyes and saw the power. Authority. Strength. The thousand-yard stare of the true combat veteran.

Petrus took her hand first, bowing slightly as he did so.

'Aunty,' he greeted. 'It is good to see you.' He turned to Garrett. 'This is my friend, Garrett.'

Garrett bowed lower and took her hand. 'It is an honor,' he said. Her hand felt like a welding glove filled with pebbles. Hard, calloused. Her grip was firm.

'I have heard of you,' she said.

Garrett smiled. 'Good things, I hope.'

She shook her head. 'No, not really.' Then she sat back down on her mustard green chair and readied the tea. She didn't ask if they wanted sugar or milk. She simply poured three mugs full, added condensed milk and a spoon of sugar. She slid one across the table to Garrett, then, with a smile, she added another three spoons of sugar to Petrus' mug and handed it to him. 'There,' she said. 'Just as you like it.'

Petrus grinned. 'Thank you, Aunty.'

'Teacher's pet,' whispered Garrett, under his breath.

Petrus assumed a look of schoolboy superiority. Smug and condescending.

Garrett covered his laughter with a cough.

'So. My boy,' continued Aunty. 'Why are you here?'

'Maybe I'm just visiting,' answered Petrus.

'Maybe,' conceded Aunty. 'But probably not.'

'Actually, Aunty,' said Petrus. 'I am looking for your help. I need a favor.'

And the Zulu told her of his brother's death, his quest for vengeance and what had happened thus far.

Afterwards, she laid a hand on his shoulder. 'I am sorry, my boy,' she said. 'The people responsible for this must pay. Your brother must be released from his earthly prison so that he can sit with his ancestors. What do you need?'

'Artillery and armor. I remember, you have a Casspir armored car and a 120mm mortar.'

Aunty Beulah's face fell. 'I am so sorry,' she said. 'I sold both of those some time back to a man in Angola.

But I still have a heavy machine gun, assault rifles, some light machine guns and a couple of 60mm mortars.'

Garrett nodded in approval. 'I know the commando mortars well. They will do, provided we have enough ammunition. Our problem is personnel. We'll need another six people, minimum.'

Aunty nodded. 'I can supply soldiers. For Petrus, a special price for the whole package. I would normally charge three hundred thousand Rands plus a sizeable deposit for this much ordinance. But I will make do with two hundred thousand.'

Petrus pulled out the large wad of cash that his father had given him. He counted it out, pilling the notes into stacks of ten thousand. There were five stacks plus a pile of loose notes.

'Just over fifty thousand,' he said.

Aunty shook her head. 'That doesn't even cover the ammunition.'

'It is all that I have,' stated Petrus.

'Then perhaps you should contact your father and ask for more,' suggested Aunty.

'Perhaps,' agreed Petrus. 'And perhaps he would send more. But bear in mind that another one hundred and fifty thousand Rands is a lot of money. If my father sent that much money then he would, most likely, send some guards with it. Perhaps even a whole impi of his warriors.'

The well-veiled threat hung in the air. Like a bad smell.

'A whole impi,' repeated Aunty.

Petrus nodded. 'Two thousand strong. Most likely. After all, he would hate to think that the murder of his youngest son was not being avenged. I am fairly sure that he would take steps to ensure that all possible help was given. It is just a thought,' he said. 'Maybe he would merely send the money. Who knows?'

Petrus was all in, and Aunty had no idea how strong his hand was.

Three minutes ticked by. The atmosphere sliced into thin manageable pieces by the clock.

Finally, Aunty spoke. The hand had gone to Petrus. 'I will have to ask for volunteers,' she said. 'For so little money I cannot order anyone to go with you. But do not worry, there are always some men who want to fight. Men like you two.'

'I have to fight,' objected Petrus. 'I must avenge my brother.'

'Yes,' she agreed. 'There is always a reason.' She looked directly at Garrett. 'A reason to let the beast out of its cage. A reason to kill. Again.'

She shook her head. Somehow, she looked much older than when they had first come in. Her face slacker. Softer. She waved a hand in dismissal. 'Go now. Wait outside. My man, Simeon, will come to you.'

The two friends left, mumbling their goodbyes on the way out.

Aunty did not reciprocate.

Once outside they found a shady spot under a stunted thorn tree and they waited.

Hours went by but Petrus advised that they simply sit down and wait. 'She has spoken,' he explained. 'To ask what is happening would be a sign of disrespect.'

'But you already disrespected her,' said Garrett. 'You threatened her with your father's army.'

Petrus shook his head. 'No. I did not threaten her. I merely reminded her of her place. It is different. I did so with respect.'

Garrett lit a cigarette and gave up trying to understand the nuances of what had just happened.

Finally, as the sun was setting, an old four-ton Bedford truck rolled into view, coughing and spluttering, smoke belching from its tailpipe. It was loaded high with sacks full of what looked like ears of corn. Sitting on top of the sacks were five men.

The truck juddered to a halt in front of Garrett and Petrus and a man climbed down from the cab.

'My name is Simeon,' he said, as he handed a sheet of paper and a pen to Petrus. 'This is the inventory. Aunty says that you must sign it.'

Petrus raised an eyebrow. 'Why? Is she going to sue me if some of the goods get scratched?'

Simeon said nothing so Petrus read the list and then scrawled his signature at the bottom.

1 x 7.62mm FN general purpose machine gun

1 x 12.7mm Browning heavy machine gun.

4 x R4 7.62mm assault rifles with 4 extra magazines

6 x Armscor hand grenades

2 x 60mm Hand held Mortar tubes

20 round high explosive mortar rounds

600 rounds 7.62 mm ammunition

500 rounds 12.7mm ammunition

'Okay,' said Petrus. 'Where is it all?'

Simon gestured towards the back of the truck. 'There, under the bags. These five men and I are your team. We are yours to command. All of us are proficient with the machine guns and the mortars.'

'Good,' acknowledged Petrus. 'Tell them to climb down. Is there a place where we can all talk?'

'My room,' answered Simeon.

They drove the Bedford behind Simeon's house and all crowded in and stood around his small kitchen table.

Garrett took a piece of paper and drew a schematic of the Russian's house and surrounds. Then he explained their method of attack.

One mortar would be placed on the koppie that he and Petrus had reconnoitered from. The heavy machine gun and the second mortar would be placed a little further away on another portion of high ground. Two of Aunty's men would man each of the weapons and one of each team would carry an R4 rifle with a full magazine.

Petrus would carry an R4 and Garrett, the general-purpose machine gun. The mortars would take out the guard huts and then lay a walking cover fire. He and Petrus would cut through the fence and head for the main house. The heavy machine gun to target all guards that try to get into the house and it would also be used to cover their retreat.

They decided to stay the night and start early the next morning.

Ten hours later, as the sun rose, the team readied themselves.

Petrus told Simeon that he was going to say good-bye to Aunty but her right hand man stopped him.

'No,' he said. 'She does not wish to see you.'

Petrus accepted what he was told and they all left. Simeon drove the Bedford, following Petrus and Garrett in the Land Cruiser.

Aunty Beulah watched them go. She knew that she was watching dead men walking. Because she knew Petrus well and, as such, it was obvious to her that his thirst for vengeance would not end today. He was man with strong beliefs, and he would keep going until he considered that every single person who had had anything to do with Malusi's death had been exterminated. The odds of him surviving were slim indeed.

As for the white man. Aunty shuddered. It had taken all of her courage to stop from trembling in fear when he had sat opposite him. For she had the gift of knowing, and when she looked at Garrett what she saw terrified her. He was less man than beast, but the will of the man was as strong as iron. And those iron bounds were all that prevented him from losing his last vestiges of humanity.

But they would break. Her vision was as clear as her eyesight on a sunny day.

Before long - the Beast would run free.

And she very much doubted that Garrett would be able to find the strength to cage it again.

CHAPTER TWENTY-TWO

The two guards laughed out loud. Bertus and Philemon had joined up with Viktor Hubenko's firm at the same time. Three months previously. Both men were in their late forties and had served in the South African Defense Force.

Both had received dishonorable discharges. One for drug dealing and the other for fraud. The exact qualities that Viktor looked for. Militarily trained with a low moral default zone.

Both agreed that it was the best thing that had ever happened to them. The pay was adequate. They gained respect from the other more nefarious elements of their society. The hours were not too odious and there were magnificent benefits.

Cheap, or sometimes free, access to drugs and drink. An impressive pool of company cars to drive and a clothing allowance so that they did not embarrass their employer when performing public close protection for him.

And then there were the girls. Viktor dealt extensively in girls and he ran a chain of houses across Johannesburg and surrounding areas. Mainly the girls were brought in from the ex-Soviet Union or Asia. They were all of a type. Young, small, pretty and innocent. None of them came of their own accord, they were all either kidnapped, sold by struggling parents or simply traded for luxury goods.

They were kept captive and immediately upon arrival were put on a course of heroin and crystal meth, causing a dependency for the drugs with a matter of days.

Then Viktor would give the girls to his guards to be "Salted", as he called it. It was true that some men would pay a premium to have a virgin but Viktor had found that to be a fairly rare occurrence. Mainly his punters wanted a girl who knew her stuff. So he encouraged his guards to push the boundaries.

'You have got to try that new Russian girl,' said Bertus. 'I promise you, she will do anything. Anything that you can dream up, as long as you promise her a syringe.'

'Really?' asked Philemon. 'So you reckon that you just lie back and she goes mad?'

'No, man,' denied Bertus irritably. 'She's got no imagination. You gotta think up the shit yourself and then tell her what to do. She's a bit slow, so sometimes you gotta smack her a bit to get her to concentrate.'

'What's her name?' asked Philemon.

'I don't fucking know,' replied Bertus. 'Why would you want to know her name? Next you'll be wanting to whisper sweet nothings in her ear when you do her.'

Philemon laughed.

'Hey,' said Bertus. 'What's that sound?'

Philemon cocked his head to one side. 'Sounds like…'

The 60mm mortar struck the guardhouse slightly to the right of center. The high explosive round detonated on impact, ripping off the ceiling and demolishing the right wall.

A chunk of masonry hit Philemon in his temple, smashing bone and brain and killing him instantly.

Bertus was not so lucky. A ragged piece of shrapnel tore off his left arm below the shoulder and the blast wave itself flayed the exposed flesh from his face. He staggered about in an ever-diminishing circle, like a dog seeking a place to rest, screaming in agony.

Finally, he fell to the floor, dying as his life's blood ebbed out of him.

The new Russian girl would not be getting her fix that night.

Both Garrett and Petrus came sprinting across the open ground, emerging from a hole that they had cut in the electric fence. All about them mortar rounds whipped through the air.

It is a common misconception propagated by Hollywood movies that when fired, mortars make a polite pop sound and then a jaunty whistle as they come down. They don't.

When a mortar bomb is launched from its firing tube there is a loud crack and an explosion of pressure.

Then the bomb travels through the air with a sound of absolute fury. A whipping, crackling scream that is almost as terrifying as the final explosion. Almost.

Two of the four guard houses were down, destroyed by mortar fire. But, by now, the final two huts had been vacated, the guards running and throwing themselves behind other available cover.

And then Garrett threw himself at Petrus, smashing him to the ground. Before the Zulu could complain, Garrett gestured towards a tripwire that they had not seen earlier.

'Careful,' he said.

Petrus nodded. 'My bad. Thanks.'

They sprang to their feet again and continued running towards the main house. Another tripwire. They hurdled it at speed.

The ground shook and bucked in cadence with the high explosive that was hammering into it. Thick dust and the smell of explosives filled the air.

Suddenly bullets spat and howled around them, the spiteful buzz of steel hornets as death plucked greedily at their clothes. Blood sprayed from Garrett's left arm as a round clipped his bicep, spinning him to the ground in a bright spray of blood.

Petrus leant down and grabbed him by his collar, dragging him to his feet.

'Where is all of this shit coming from?' shouted Garrett.

Petrus pointed at the flat roof of the main house. A row of heavily armed men was standing on the roof firing at them.

Abruptly the mortar bombs stopped falling.

'They're out of ammo,' yelled Petrus.

Inside Garrett's mind, the beast threw itself at the steel doors that penned it in, snarling and howling. He raised his machine gun and pulled the trigger, dragging it along the roofline. Chips of brick and tile exploded into the air and the shooters dived for cover. One of them didn't move fast enough and the stream of high velocity steel picked him up and threw him off the roof like a rag doll involved in a child's tantrum.

Five more guards ran at them, coming from the perimeter of the property. Petrus laid down fire while Garrett continued blasting away at the roof.

The new guards were practicing fire and movement, covering each other as they inched forward. Their shots were controlled, well aimed. Their movements spoke of training and experience.

'Shit,' said Garrett. 'These guys are pretty good.'

Then the 12.7mm Browning heavy machine gun opened up. The sound a chorus of kettledrums. Fast booming percussion. The devil's drum solo.

All about the guards, the earth simply disintegrated as the half-inch bullets punched through them, tearing them asunder and painting the dusty earth with their blood. Chewing them up and spitting them out.

Garrett stood up and continued running towards the house, firing from the hip as he did.

The belt of ammunition flipped over his shoulder as it fed into the ever-hungry maw of the squad support weapon, hammering out death at ten rounds per second. As it ran dry, Garrett ripped a grenade from his pocket, pulled the pin and threw it onto the roof. It exploded with a sharp magnesium crack and filled the air with hundreds of steel flechettes.

'Cover me while I reload,' he shouted.

Petrus shouldered his rifle and snapped off rounds at anything moving. Garrett dropped to one knee and fed another belt into the machine gun, slamming the receiver shut and cycling it before he stood up.

They ran for the door. Garrett fired at the hinges and they crashed into it together, smashing the door into the room.

Three men inside shooting at them. A bullet grazed Petrus' thigh and the Zulu went down hard, rolling as he hit the floor.

Garrett stood firm and raked the men with a long burst. The bullets tore into them, dancing them backwards as they jerked from side to side. Machine gun marionettes.

Petrus got back up and the two of them ran to the entrance of the corridor. Checked. A grenade came rolling down towards them.

'Incoming,' shouted Garrett. The two of them retreated and grabbed the broken door, pulling it over them for cover. The grenade exploded with a sharp crack and bits of shrapnel punched through the door as if it wasn't even there.

Garrett and Petrus gave themselves the once over, checking for holes. Nothing. Relief.

Men coming down the corridor. Firing. Both Garrett and Petrus opened up and the men flew back in a welter of blood and gore.

They could hear the 12.7mm outside, still playing its opus of death as it hosed down the house with steel. Shattered roof tiles rained down and bits of the ceiling started to fall into the house as the Browning chewed the building up.

And then, silence.

'They're out,' said Petrus. 'We're on our own.'

They ran down the corridor. Working room to room. Kicking doors open, firing. Next room, shouldering the door open, stepping inside.

There were four girls in the room. Dressed only in the skimpiest of lace panties. They were young. Their skin should have shone with the blossom of youth but instead it was sallow. Bruised. Their eyes were vacant, underneath were dark circles. Arms a wasteland of ragged tracks left by needles.

The oldest could not have been more than seventeen. She looked closer to forty.

Used needles were scattered carelessly on the floor and the room stank of sweat and sex. Garrett looked the oldest one in the eyes. They were blank. Lifeless. A walking corpse. Mere grist for the mill. A life brought low by the greed of evil men.

And finally, The Beast broke free.

Garrett's vision blurred as sweat ran into his eyes. His ears rang from the percussive abuse. He was back in Sierra Leone. Or Sudan. Algeria. Djibouti. Mali.

The air thick with the smell of death. A combination of blood and sweat and cordite and smoke and dust. It coated the back of their throats like diesel oil. Sickening. Cloying. Intoxicating.

A tonic for The Beast. The manna on which it fed.

The machine-gun chattered again. Insane laughter. Two men died. Three more entered the corridor from the side. But The Beast was amongst them, and it screamed incoherently as it killed, firing at point blank range. Tearing them in half with its steel jacketed talons.

They entered the last room.

One man. Sitting at a desk, in front of him a gun. A gold-plated Colt 45, tricked out with all of the extras. Compensator, laser sites, Pachmayr grips, extended magazine. A pimp's guns. Impractical. More bling than weapon.

The beast threw its head back and howled.

Petrus flinched at the inhuman sound.

The man behind the desk went pale and raised his hands above his head.

Garrett stared at him. Wild eyed. Machine gun rock steady in his hand.

Petrus put his hand on his shoulder. 'Don't shoot him,' he said. 'We need to talk.'

Garrett looked at the Zulu, his eyes full of contempt. Bereft of recognition. Animal. And then a flicker and he was back. There but barely controlled.

He nodded.

Petrus let out a soft sigh of relief.

The man at the desk did not move. He appeared to be totally expressionless, but that was only because of his shaved his head. Not just his hair, his eyebrows as well. It gave him a look of a recovered cancer patient, or burn victim. Blank and featureless.

'Are you Viktor Hubenko?' asked Petrus.

The man nodded.

'Where are your three sidekicks? The other three Russians.'

'Fuck you,' said Viktor. 'I'm not Russian. I'm Ukrainian.'

Petrus cuffed him on the side of the head. 'I don't care - where are the other three?'

'Dead,' replied Viktor. 'You killed them, you crazy fucks. Who are you? Who do you work for?'

Petrus ignored the questions. 'Do you deal in rhino horn?'

Viktor shrugged.

Petrus hit him again. This time harder.

'Okay, yes,' admitted Viktor. 'I collect it for some yellow bastard. Why? You want some?' He sneered. 'You need to make your dick hard?'

Petrus hit him again. This time a solid backhand that brought a reward of bright red blood from the Ukrainian's nose.

'How do you collect it?

'From the Kruger. We go, we shoot them, we harvest the horns. What are you, some sort of green activist? What the fuck do you care where I get the horns from?'

'I care since you killed my brother to do it.'

Viktor looks at Petrus for a while. 'I'm sorry. It wasn't personal. It's business, that's all.'

The Zulu raised his hand and Viktor flinched but Petrus didn't strike. Instead, he asked another question.

'Who do you supply the horns to?'

'What does it matter?' Asked Viktor. 'Your brother is dead. All my men are dead.'

'It matters,' said Petrus, his voice low. Expressionless.

Viktor shook his head. 'No, it doesn't matter. Fuck you.'

Petrus hit him again.

'Hit me all you want. Shoot me. I don't care, it's all over. Fuck the both of you. Fuck you all and this shitty country and your stupid rhinos.'

Petrus calmly put down his rifle and drew his assegai from his shoulder sheath.

'What now?' asked Viktor. 'You going to stab me? Big fucking deal. Go for it, kill me,' he sneered.

Petrus struck the Ukrainian in the temple with the butt of his assegai. The he dragged him, semi-unconscious, over the desk and, using the razor-sharp blade, he sliced off his trousers, cutting deeply into his legs as he did so.

Then he sliced the trousers into lengths, spread-eagled Viktor on his back across the desk and tied each leg and each arm to one of the desk's four legs.

Viktor shook his head as he slowly rose back to consciousness.

'I'm not going to kill you,' said Petrus.

'Oh, well that's mighty big of you,' sneered Viktor. 'Why not?'

'My brother's spirit walks alone in the darkness,' said Petrus. 'He is unable to sit with his ancestors, unable to find eternal peace until I avenge his death. And his death is only avenged when I decide that it is avenged. Killing you and your men is not enough. All who were involved must pay. Before he can find rest in peace the very earth must be expunged of the vileness that caused his death. All of it - every single person involved must be crushed. So - I say again. Whom do you supply the horns to?'

Viktor grinned, the expression at odds with the blankness of his shaved head. 'Do what you want,' he said. And then, almost as an afterthought. 'Fuck you and your brother.'

Petrus nodded. 'Hard man, mister Hubenko,' he said as he leant forward and, using the flat of his assegai blade, he lifted up Viktor's genitals.

'Hey,' yelled the Ukrainian. 'Careful. What are you doing?'

Petrus flicked the blade. A tiny movement that involved only the smallest turn of his wrist. A thumbnail sized piece of flesh flew off followed by a thin jet of blood.

The Ukrainian screamed.

'Don't panic,' said Petrus. 'I haven't cut your horn off. It's just a small flesh wound.'

Viktor sagged with relief.

'But make no mistake,' continued Petrus. 'I am going to cut it off. The whole lot.'

He flicked the big man's penis and then slid the blade across his scrotum. Viktor's stomach cramped with fear, his abdominals standing out like pebbles on a beach.

'Then I'm going to heat my blade up,' continued Petrus. 'And use it to cauterize the wound. Make sure that you don't bleed to death. That's all - no more, no less. So, your choice. You squat to piss for the rest of your life or you talk.'

He grabbed Viktor's face. 'Look at me. Do you believe me?'

Viktor nodded.

'Say it,' shouted Petrus.

'I believe.'

'Louder.'

'I believe.'

'With feeling,' yelled Petrus as he flicked the blade again.

'I believe,' screamed Viktor. 'Jesus Christ, I believe. Don't, please don't. Jesus fuck. His name is Jin Chang. Colonel Jin Chang, Chinese army, based in Zimbabwe, Harare. We meet him in Zimbabwe, Beit Bridge. He waits for us there; sometimes it's his aide, a sergeant Lu Feng. We supply the shipment; he pays us in uncut diamonds. It pays well…really well. As I said - it's just business. Nothing personal. Nothing.'

'Who else is involved?' asked Petrus.

'That's all. I swear. I don't know what he does with it or where it goes. I don't ask I don't care. He pays, we go.'

'Jin Chang, you say?'

'Yes,' agreed Viktor. 'Jin Chang. Colonel. Zimbabwe. Beit Bridge.'

Petrus spun the assegai in his hand and stared at the Russian for a while. Finally, he said. 'I believe you.'

'Thank you,' gasped Viktor.

'But it is personal. You killed my brother. It doesn't get more personal than that.'

Viktor took a deep breath. 'Make it quick,' he said. 'I beg of you.'

Petrus moved like lightning striking. The assegai fluted through the air and Viktor's head leapt from his shoulders and struck the wall. A jet of blood arced across the room.

A monochromatic gateway painted with Death's gruesome hand.

The two friends left via the destroyed front door. All about them lay the dead. Pools of dark, sticky blood. Flies. Smoking holes in the ground. Hundreds of bright brass cartridges scattered like corn seeds. Or chicken feed.

And in his mental cage of steel and willpower, the Beast smiled in grim satisfaction.

In the long grass, in deep shadow and not moving, lay Stas. The sole survivor. A rough tourniquet tied around his leg and another bloody scrap of material wound around his head.

They walked by close enough for him to hear Petrus.

'We need to get to Harare as soon as. Sort this colonel Chang out.'

He marked the two attackers well and waited for them to disappear before he moved.

CHAPTER TWENTY-THREE

L u Feng sat in the front of the APC, waiting for one of the Ukrainians to arrive with the latest shipment. Next to him was a driver. In the back, fifteen of his special-forces troops. The APC was parked on the outskirts of the little town of Beit Bridge.

Sergeant Feng hated the little town of Beit Bridge. He also hated the large town of Harare.

And the country that it was in.

And the continent that surrounded it.

Whereas colonel Jin Chang was an Afrophile, sergeant Feng was more of an Afro-fuck-off.

He missed China. He missed his family.

He supposed that he should have been more grateful for his posting. Particularly his teaming up with colonel Chang. As a result of his nefarious activities, he now earned over twenty times what an actual master sergeant would earn. More than a hundred times what his father earned. He sent home all of the money that he could afford to. His family were far and away the wealthiest in their village because of him.

He particularly missed his older sister, Mengzu. She was two years older than him and his parents were lucky enough to live in a rural region where the one child policy was laxer than the more urban areas, allowing a second child when the first one was a female.

Lu Feng had not actually spoken to any members of his family for over six years. He did write every three to six months. Letters painstakingly drawn with poor hand and containing little news, due to the draconian Chinese system of censorship.

They would reply with a letter that had obviously been prepared by a professional scribe with flowing hand and full of praise and stilted honorifics.

He waited all day until the sun sank behind the horizon in a solar display of reds and purples and golds. No one arrived. It was the first meeting that the Ukrainians had ever missed.

The sergeant decided to book into the only hotel in the town, leaving his men to sleep rough under or around the APC.

The next day he waited until midday and then decided that he would have to call a no show and head back to Harare. He was not looking forward to telling the colonel. He knew that the colonel would lose it, scream and shout and rant. He would blame Lu Feng. Just as he blamed him for everything from the heat, to the rain, to the fucking flies.

The master sergeant sighed. Once again, he wished that he were home again - looking at the Huangshan Mountains, talking to his older sister, eating proper food instead of inelegant lumps of meat and porridge.

And not being blamed for every single thing that went wrong.

CHAPTER TWENTY-FOUR

Garrett and Petrus had returned to Natal to plan for the next part of their quest. Now they stood next to Malusi's grave.

Petrus had told his brother what had transpired so far. He also asked if Malusi remembered Garrett, and explained that the soldier was helping.

The Zulu sent for beer and the two friends sat down next to the grave. They drank. They smoked.

They spoke.

For the first time, Petrus asked Garrett for details about his home life. Who exactly he worked for, where he lived. Did he have cattle?

'I live in the Scottish Highlands,' said Garrett. 'On a farm owned by The Much Honored, The Laird of Halgowan.'

'Laird?'

'Like a chief,' explained Garrett. 'A landowner of great consequence. I have known him since I was a child. After my parents died, when I was young, he took me in. Paid for my boarding school. Gave me a place to stay after...' Garrett paused for thought. 'Well...after,' he concluded.

'I see,' nodded Petrus. 'So, does he have many Impi?'

Garrett shook his head. 'No. He has about fifty staff. No Impi.'

'Just you?'

Garrett nodded. 'Just me.'

'Well then he is adequately protected,' admitted Petrus. 'Much cattle?'

Garrett nodded. 'Much cattle. Big, fat, plentiful. It is a gentle land. Very green. It rains much of the time. In the winter it snows.'

'I have seen snow,' said Petrus. 'High in the mountains in Lesotho. I did not like it.' He lit another cigarette. 'So, do the other tribes try to steal your cattle?'

'No,' said Garrett. 'Once we had a little trouble with poachers but I sorted that out.'

'You killed them?'

Garrett laughed. 'You can't simply kill people there. It's different to here. They would call that murder and they take that very seriously.'

'Here as well,' said Petrus. 'But you just hide the bodies. No problem.'

'Can't do that in Scotland,' said Garrett. 'If they suspect a murder, they put one hundred, maybe two hundred police onto it. And they stay on the case until they solve it.'

Petrus raised an eyebrow. 'You don't say?' He shook his head. 'I have a friend who used to work with the

Durban CID. Detective. Sometimes he used to have over three hundred murder dockets open at the same time. They have to declare a cold case after a few days. Solve it or move on before you get buried in murder cases.' The Zulu thought for a while. Contemplating what it would be like to live with such lawfulness. He decided that he wouldn't enjoy it much.

'Tell me then, Garrett,' he continued. 'In this gentle place - is there racism?'

'Yes,' admitted the soldier.

'Why?' asked Petrus. 'Was there apartheid?'

'No.'

'So why the racism?'

'I don't know why, I really don't. You get stupid people everywhere.'

Petrus cocked his head to one side. 'I don't mind racism. I don't like most people. Most races. It is hard being a Zulu - we are so superior to everybody else that racism seems to be a natural default setting.'

The two of them sat in silence for a while and then Garrett burst out laughing.

Petrus joined in. They laughed for ages. An outlet of emotion. A catharsis.

Their mirth was interrupted by one of the tribal elders. He handed Petrus an envelope. Petrus thanked him and he left.

'When this is all over, if we are still amongst the living,' said Petrus. 'I would like to come to this

Scotland of yours. Pay tribute to your chief. Drink beer and see some more snow.'

'That would be good,' said Garrett. 'That would be very good.'

Petrus took the contents of the envelope out. It was a used South African passport. He flicked it open. Inside was a picture of Garrett. They had decided that it would be more prudent to organize Garrett a South African passport, rather than apply for a visa to get into Zimbabwe. So Petrus' father had simply ordered one of his subjects to volunteer up his passport and then his photo was changed for one of Garrett.

Now Garrett had a genuine passport in the name of Dingane Zondi.

Petrus handed it to the soldier. Garrett looked at it with some skepticism. 'Dingane Zondi. Really?'

'It's just a name,' said Petrus.

'What's in a name,' quoted Garrett. 'That which we call a rose by any other name would smell as sweet.'

'Yeah, whatever,' countered Petrus. 'Just say that your father was a Zulu.'

The next morning, they loaded the pickup with food and water and a change of clothes and started their drive to Zimbabwe.

They carried no weapons bar the assegai and the machete. The plan was to source weapons once they were in country and Petrus had an address that they would need to visit to do so. They also took another thick wad of US Dollars.

They hit the blacktop highway at the same time that the sun rose, bathing the land with an urgent red and orange glow. A heart of fire transfusing the land with its own blood.

Garrett kept the pick up at ten miles over the speed limit and it ate up the road with ease. They stopped for gas at midday and then continued on with Petrus behind the wheel. The miles spooled by as they left KwaZulu and entered the Free State, South Africa's equivalent of the Midwest. Mile after mile of flat land filled with corn and grain broken only by the odd massive concrete grain silo.

'You know,' said Petrus. 'Back in the days of Apartheid, Indians were not allowed to stay overnight in the Free State. Transit only.'

'Why?' asked Garrett.

'Who knows? A lot of weird laws back then,' Petrus stared out of the window for a while as the miles of nothing continued to reel past. 'Not much of a hardship,' he said. 'I mean, who the fuck would want to live here anyway?'

Half an hour later they drove past a town called Bethlehem.

'Check it out,' said Petrus. 'Just like the Bible. Except no wise men. Lots of virgins though.'

Garrett chuckled.

That night they stayed at the Ingwe Motel close to the border between South Africa and Zimbabwe. Garrett had stayed in prisons that had been more comfortable. And cleaner. So he had no argument when Petrus insisted that they rise at four thirty that morning so as to get an early start at the border. They arrived at half past six and there was already a queue that promised to take anywhere between five to seven hours to be processed.

However, Petrus parked the pick up on the side of the road and walked to the customs office with a case of whisky and a small sheaf of US Dollars.

Two hours later they were escorted through the border post by a captain who was now richer both in dollars and alcoholic beverages.

The two friends drove to the town of Beit Bridge and set about gaining some intel by the simple and straight forward method of approaching people in the street. Offering them some money and then asking questions. It was a small town, and the fact that Petrus was offering fifty-dollar notes to people in a country where the average daily income was less than six dollars, all combined to provide a wealth of detailed information.

Less than an hour there was a substantial queue of people standing outside Petrus' and Garrett's pick up waiting to tell all that they knew. Petrus walked down the queue and, using a method based primarily on age and sex, reduced it to four people. All male, all aged thirty to forty.

'Why these guys?' asked Garrett.

'Young kids are pointless,' answered Petrus. 'They don't really know the subtleties of what's going on. Old people are often lonely so they want to talk more. They'll waste our time.'

'And women?'

'I can't threaten a woman if I don't believe her,' said Petrus. 'So. Men, middle aged, probably have families to support, more likely to tell you something that they shouldn't because they're more desperate for the money.'

Garrett nodded. 'There I was thinking that it was just good old-fashioned sexism and ageism.'

Petrus looked offended. He called up the first person and asked if they knew of the Russians, colonel Jin Chang and his sergeant, Lu Feng.

It so happened that everybody seemed to know of all three parties. For some reason the locals called colonel Jin Chang, The General and they called sergeant Lu Feng, The Captain. But aside from their inadvertent promotional practices it was obvious that they were talking about the same people. The Ukrainians were simply known as, the foreigners or the Russians.

It was the fourth man who offered up a batch of additional information.

'The Captain is a nice man,' he said. 'But The General is a big prick, he looks on us as though we are less than dogs. Sometimes they come together, but normally only The Captain comes. They always come with a truck of soldiers and sometimes two trucks. Smart soldiers not like the Zimbabwe soldiers.'

'Chinese soldiers?' asked Petrus.

'Yes,' said the informer. 'Dark camouflage, a round cap with a sword and lightening.'

Garrett looked up. 'Do they have a red flag above the patch?'

The man thought for a few seconds and then nodded.

'Oh shit,' exclaimed Garrett. 'Those are Nanjing Flying Tiger Special Forces troops. Bad bastards all. No one in their right mind wants to fuck with those guys.'

Petrus laughed. 'It's just as well that we're not in our right minds then,' he quipped.

But Garrett didn't join in with his friend's laughter as he wondered just how far they could keep pushing their luck. When would it run out with fatal consequences for the both of them?

Still chuckling, Petrus paid off the informer and the two of them climbed into the car, ready to travel to Harare.

CHAPTER TWENTY-FIVE

They booked into the Crowne Plaza Monomatapa Hotel. A three-star hotel in Park Lane, Harare. It was clean and cheap.

The next morning, they woke and ate a breakfast of gargantuan proportions. Eggs, bacon, steak, lamb chops, liver, fries, toast and coffee. A feast of plenty in a country where over half of the population were literally starving to death.

After the meal they drove to the suburb of Avondale, to meet with their contact at his house.

When they arrived at the house, the front gate was already open and there was a water truck parked in the driveway. Attached to the truck was a hose that led to a large PVC tank. This was because, even though hundreds of millions of dollars had been borrowed from the World Bank to upgrade the country's water. No money had actually been spent on any water projects and so potable water was now a luxury, as opposed to a basic human right. For those who could afford it, water deliveries were the only way to go.

Garrett and Petrus waited until the delivery had been completed and the truck left, then they drove in and parked while the automatic gate closed behind them.

Their contact was a Greek man, Roddy Dukakis, who had been born in Athens but had immigrated to Zimbabwe in the seventies when it was still known as Rhodesia. He had been a member of the Rhodesian army, not as a combat soldier but as a sergeant in the quarter master division.

At the end of the war, when the Rhodesian army was disbanded, he had taken advantage of the chaos and literally stolen truck loads of weapons, ammunition, generators, uniforms, tents and food rations. Initially he had done a great trade to local warlords as well as mercenaries, both local and up through Africa. But, as time went on and his equipment became more and more outdated, his business fell off. And now only the most desperate used him.

Garrett and Petrus were firmly in the most desperate camp.

After the usual greeting and small talk, including a tiny cup of the strongest coffee that Garrett had ever tasted, Roddy led them to his strong room. They went through a false door concealed behind his refrigerator, down into his basement.

Inside there was a treasure trove of outdated, but still useable weapons, dating from the sixties and seventies.

Petrus waved Garrett forward, relying on the soldier's expertise to make the best of a fairly limited choice.

It didn't take Garrett long before he had a pile of arms and munitions on the central wooden table.

Two FN FAL Belgian assault rifles, circa 1965 complete with wooden furniture and 7.62mm twenty round steel magazines. Weighing in at twelve pounds when fully loaded as opposed to the M16 that weighs in at only 7 pounds.

A Bren Mk 4 chambered for the 7.62mm round. Thirty round magazines and a whopping thirty pounds in weight.

A Couple of Browning High Power's in 9 x 19mm parabellum with thirteen round magazines.

A box of twenty x M26 fragmentation grenades

Ten M18 Claymore mines - little three-pound packages of death. Each filled with 680 grams of C4 explosive packed around seven hundred steel balls. Deadly up to a range of two hundred and fifty yards.

Then Petrus spotted an old M20 Superbazooka. A sixty-inch aluminium tube capable of firing a ten-pound high explosive projectile for a distance in excess of 1000 yards.

'I want that,' said the Zulu, attracted, as per usual, by the sheer size of the weapon. 'And I'm going to stick it right up colonel Chang's ass and pull the trigger.'

Garrett placed it on the table along with five high explosive bombs for same.

Finally, a case of sixteen blocks of C4 explosive complete with a selection of pencil detonators in different times, extra magazines for all of the weapons and two thousand rounds of ammunition.

Roddy looked at the haul. 'Ten thousand dollars American,' he said.

Garrett shook his head. 'No way, man. This is museum stuff. We'll give you five.'

Roddy grabbed at his chest like he was having a heart attack. 'No, no, no,' he gasped. 'These are good weapons. The best. Eight thousand.'

'Six thousand,' countered Garrett.

'Seven thousand five hundred,' stated Roddy. 'And that is it. No negations. Already you have stolen money from the mouths of my children.'

'You don't have kids,' said Petrus.

Roddy shrugged. 'Figuratively speaking. I tell you what, I'll throw in that old WWII Mk5 antitank mine.'

Garrett nodded and put his hand out. They shook and Petrus counted out the cash.

Then they carried the lot up the stairs and loaded it into the false bottom of the pickup.

Roddy watched the two men leave and, as they did so, he let out a sigh of relief. He hadn't quite realized, up until that point, how nervous the two men had made him feel. It was like being locked in a room with two pit bulls and a piece of steak. You knew that you would be fine for a while. But as soon as the steak had been consumed, you knew that you would be the next thing on the menu.

He closed the door behind him and went to make himself another coffee.

As it percolated, he sat and thought. He had heard the Zulu mention colonel Chang.

Roddy knew the colonel. Everybody knew the colonel. He also could not stand the colonel. Then again, no one could stand the colonel.

But there was no denying that Jin Chang was the seat of power in the region. A corrupt man short on morality and big on influence. And he would not stand a double cross of any sort. In fact, if word ever got out that Roddy had supplied the men that went after Jin Chang, then the Greek could kiss his slightly-better-than-mediocre life goodbye.

And it would be a long and painful departure indeed.

He decided to finish his coffee and then he would phone the colonel. Make sure that he was on his good side.

CHAPTER TWENTY-SIX

Stas arrived at the Harare International airport early Wednesday morning. He joined the crew at the taxi rank, took one straight to the Chinese embassy and asked for colonel Jin Chang.

The receptionist told him to wait in the atrium.

Five hours later he was still waiting.

Eventually sergeant Feng arrived. He did not speak to Stas, he merely beckoned for him to follow. They walked out of the building and got into a black Mercedes S500. Lu Feng drove and Stas sat in the passenger seat.

Although he tried to draw the sergeant into a conversation, Lu Feng did not react and they spent the entire trip in silence.

They pulled up at a pair of electric gates that barred access to a magnificent mansion in Borrowdale, one of the more up market suburbs of Harare. Feng used a remote control to buzz the gates open and they crunched up the long, gravel driveway.

The sergeant led Stas through the house to the colonel's study.

The colonel was standing behind his desk, his body stiff with controlled rage. 'Why did you go to the embassy, you stupid fuck?' he asked.

'You watch your mouth, you yellow prick,' answered Stas, thrusting his face aggressively close to the colonel.

Chang cuffed the Ukrainian across his face and sergeant Feng immediately drew his pistol and pointed it at Stas.

'You stupid moron,' continued the colonel. 'Are you deliberately trying to destroy this business? I'm warning you, if you continue missing meetings and coming to the embassy then you will fuck it all up. Well and truly.'

Stas smirked. 'Well your warning has come a little late, colonel,' he said. 'I'm here to tell you that the business is already well and truly fucked.'

Chang paused his tirade. 'What do you mean?'

'There is no more business,' continued Stas. 'There is no more anything. We were attacked two days ago. Everyone is dead. Yarik, Igor, all of the guards. The buildings have been blown up, the cars shot to shit. They beheaded Viktor. It was a fucking blood bath.'

Jin Chang went pale. His face immediately glazed over with a thin sheen of cold sweat. 'Who attacked? How many?'

Stas looked shifty, his eyes casting around the room as he thought. 'I'm not sure,' he said. 'Lots. Maybe fifty people. Maybe more.'

'Fifty?' asked the colonel. 'That many?'

'Maybe more. They had artillery and machine guns. Hi Tech stuff. We didn't stand a chance. Maybe even armored vehicles.'

'Maybe armored vehicles,' scoffed the colonel. 'You can't miss armored vehicles. Either they had them or they didn't.'

'They did,' said Stas. 'A few of them.'

Chang turned and faced out of the window, not to look at the view of the garden but merely to gather himself. To think. His brain was close to shutting down at the immensity of the Ukrainian's news. His entire future was hanging in the balance.

'Who could it be?' he asked. 'Who would dare?' He turned back to face the two men. 'Who cuts off heads as a warning?'

'Mexicans,' offered sergeant Feng. 'Muslims.'

'Mexicans,' said Chang. 'What are you, fucking simple? Might be Muslims though. Shit, that's all that we need. Bloody religious fanatics. Could be another Triad. Could be the Russians - they hate the Ukrainians. Mind you, could be any of the eastern bloc gangs, they all have the muscle and the will.'

'The Nigerians?' suggested Stas.

'Not their style,' answered Chang. 'They're more into the con than full on military action.'

'South Africans?' ventured sergeant Feng. 'The older crowd. Ex-military.'

The colonel rubbed his eyes. 'I hope not. I truly do. But that makes sense. It would explain the weapons, the armor. The ferocity of the attack. Ex-SA military, right wing fanatics muscling into the rhino trade. This is not good. Not good at all. I'm going to have to tell Tai Zeng and he is not going to be happy. Anyway,' continued the colonel. 'I'm sure that we shall never find out who it was. Probably some local gang war. Fighting for territory or control of the local drugs market.'

'There is one more thing,' said Stas as he tried to hide the look of satisfaction on his face. 'I heard them mention you. They said that they were coming for you. Here, in Harare.'

Jin Chang felt a tremor of fear ripple through him. 'Sergeant,' he barked. 'I want the men on full alert. Rotate in eight-hour shifts, issue extra ammunition. Now.'

The two men left the room and the colonel sat down behind his desk. He was so far out of his comfort zone that he was almost in a different dimension. He had always dealt from a position of strength, one of nature's natural bullies. And now he had an unknown enemy with a force that, by all accounts, exceeded his.

And they cut people's heads off.

Waves of nausea surged through him as the full consequence of what he had just been told struck home.

With Viktor's operation being no more, it meant, for the foreseeable future, eighty percent of his income had ceased. Without that income he could ill afford to pay the bribes that he needed, to keep the rest of his businesses going. So, the harsh reality was that, to all intents and purposes, his current reign of power was over.

No more Yi Deng Bo or chief of the first rank. And with no funds coming in to pay his special force soldiers, they would most certainly stick to the letter of martial law. They would obey him as a colonel but no longer as an employer.

However - he did have savings. In fact, he had a vast fortune in uncut diamonds and in cash. American dollars. Perhaps it was time to step away from the table and cash in his winnings. Time to do something else. Or at very least, do the same thing but somewhere else.

Now he just had to work out what to do, how to do it, and how to stay alive at the same time.

Then the phone rang. Chang stared at it for a long while, willing it to stop. He simply felt like he didn't have the strength to deal with anything else.

Eventually he picked it up.

It was Roddy the Greek.

The call was short and to the point and when it was over, colonel Chang was even more puzzled than he had been before.

'A white man and a Zulu,' he murmured. 'Who are these two?' he asked himself. 'Are they assassins? A recce for the main force?'

Chang went to his liquor cabinet and helped himself to a large tumbler of Johnny Walker Blue Label. No water, no ice. He needed to feel the burn as the alcohol coursed down his throat. He needed it to burn his mind clear.

He needed a game plan. It was time to call in some favors. Or at least one favor. He picked up his phone and dialed a cell number. He was one of the very few people who had access to that specific number. In fact, not even the woman's husband knew it.

It rang a few times and then it was answered. As was her habit she said nothing. Simply switching the phone on and waiting, the only sound, her breathing.

So Chang spoke first, greeting her in the manner that she preferred, even though, strictly speaking, the form of address was incorrect.

'Good evening, Madam President,' he said.

'Colonel,' she answered.

Chang took a deep breath. This woman was very difficult to deal with, he reminded himself. She drove a hard bargain, she gave nothing away, she was utterly ruthless, completely amoral and totally untrustworthy. But she owed colonel Chang.

After the United Kingdom had indefinitely frozen all of Mugabe's overseas assets and accounts and banned him and Grace from entering the United Kingdom, Tai Zeng had advised colonel Chang to approach missus Mugabe with a view to setting up a pipeline. Through this she could still move money out of Zimbabwe and into private accounts set up under dummy corporations, totally untraceable back to either herself or her husband.

She had agreed, with two major provisos - it would all be in her name and her husband was not to know about it.

And so, over the last few years, Chang had helped Grace Mugabe, via the transportation of uncut diamonds, rhino horn, ivory and drugs, to build up a retirement fund. She currently controlled five accounts in various Hong Kong banks. The total sum of all accounts combined was a little under One Billion United States Dollars.

The forty-four-year-old ex-secretary was one of Africa's wealthiest people. In fact, she had become one of the wealthiest women in the entire world.

And a large part of her wealth was due to Chang's advice. So, the colonel told her his problem and asked for her help.

There was a long pause before she answered. Then finally.

'If something happened to you, colonel,' she said. 'It would prove to be…inconvenient. I will take steps.'

She disconnected the call without saying goodbye.

Chang poured himself another whisky. He wasn't sure what Grace Mugabe would do, but he was sure of one thing, she would not want her golden pipeline to disappear, so she would be doing something.

CHAPTER TWENTY-SEVEN

Garrett and Petrus waited until darkness before they ventured out from the hotel. Both of them wore long khaki cotton dustcoats. Long riders.

The coats were thin enough for the hot weather and long enough to conceal their FN assault rifles that they had slung from their shoulders, nestled in under their arms.

They drove the pick up to the outskirts of the suburb of Borrowdale and then proceeded on foot towards Chang's residence, ostensibly for reconnaissance but also willing to take advantage of any targets of opportunity. In other words, if they saw colonel Chang, they were most likely, going to shoot him.

Garrett had picked up a map at a local gas station. It was old and out of date but it got them into the general area and, after a couple of wrong turns, they found the colonel's house.

It was a mansion. Built in a Southern Antebellum style with a sweeping in-out driveway and a landscaped garden, it was at once both ostentatious and breath taking.

The two friends picked a house on the opposite side of the road and three down from the colonel. It seemed to be uninhabited at the moment, although the garden was still being maintained, so it was likely that the owners were simply on holiday.

There was a huge mango tree in the front yard, leafy and large boughed. Garrett and Petrus shinned up into the top part of the tree and Garrett pulled out a small pair of binoculars to check out their target. He scanned slowly from left to right.

'Eight guards,' he said. 'All very visible. Definitely Flying Tiger Special Forces. Carrying the QBZ-95 rifle. Bullpup, 5.8x42mm rounds. Sidearms. No grenades.'

After another ten minutes he turned to Petrus. 'There's something wrong here,' he said as he passed the binoculars over to his friend. 'Check out the top floor windows on the right.'

Petrus did so.

'What do you see?' asked Garrett.

'Looks like people. Hard to tell. Shapes.'

'How many?'

'Not sure,' answered Petrus. 'Two rooms. Maybe eight or ten people in each room. They look crowded.'

'I think that it's the rest of his Special Forces guys. He's billeting them in his house.'

'That's unusual,' remarked Petrus.

'Unheard of,' said Garrett.

'So why is he doing it?'

Garrett thought for a moment. 'He knows that we're coming for him,' he said. 'Someone ratted us out.'

'Roddy the Greek,' said Petrus.

'Not necessarily,' disagreed Garrett. 'Could have been someone from Beit Bridge. An informer from South Africa. Who knows? The upshot is, there are a shitload of Flying Tigers in there, between thirty and forty. And they're ready for us.'

'So, what do we do now?' asked Petrus.

'These guys are good,' said Garrett. 'China have the biggest army in the world so they get a lot of choice. These dudes are the best of the best chosen from a population of almost half the world.'

'Are they as good as us?'

Garrett thought for a while. It was a serious question and now was not the time for false modesty. Now was the time for truth. 'No,' he answered. 'They aren't. But there are over thirty of them. So, I would say that we are reasonably outnumbered. A frontal attack would be suicide. We have to think this one through.'

'So think,' said Petrus.

Garrett grinned. 'I'll do so,' and he lifted the binoculars back up to continue his surveillance.

After ten minutes he put the binoculars back in his coat pocket.

'Come on,' he said to Petrus. 'We need to take a closer look.'

The two of them skirted colonel Chang's house, cutting through his neighbors' residences and climbing any convenient trees to gain a different sightline. As usual they both moved with animal like stealth, merging with the shadows. At one with the darkness.

After they had finished a full circuit Garrett patted Petrus on the shoulder and gestured for him to follow. They snuck back to their vehicle, firstly placing their FN's back into the hidden compartment and then getting in. They did not speak until they were actually inside.

'So,' said Petrus. 'You got any semblance of a plan?'

Garrett nodded. 'I have. But it's a bit of a Hail Mary pass. We can't take him in his house. Even if we get in, the odds will be so far against us that we would be pretty certain of not getting out. I reckon that we have more of a chance if we can move him. Or at least, get him to move himself. Now, the only way that we can do that is to make him feel less than safe where he is. I say that we lay a bunch of C4 shaped charges on his wall, blow a few holes in them. If we lay them correctly the blast will all go inwards so there's little chance of collateral damage to the neighbors. Then we fire a round or two of the superbazooka, maybe we even hit him, who knows, then we run like hell. My feeling is that he will move to a safer haven. One with fewer holes in the wall and fewer bomb-damaged rooms. Then we either try to get him when he's on the move or we simply reassess the situation and try again.'

'It's workable,' admitted Petrus.

'Good,' agreed Garrett. 'So. Let's go back to the hotel. Get a feed and maybe a couple of hours sleep. Come back and begin at two or three in the morning.'

Petrus nodded and Garrett started up the pickup and pulled into the road, switching on the headlamps as he did so. He turned right and then left into Borrowdale Road and drove past the racecourse, heading down the long straight road towards the town center.

Petrus noticed it first and pointed ahead. 'What's that?' he asked. 'Some sort of road block?'

Garrett peered into the darkness. It appeared to be a hastily thrown up blockade. Two vehicles parked across the road and a single traffic cone.

'Cops?' questioned Petrus.

'I don't think so,' answered Garrett as he slowed down. 'Looks like military jeeps. Army.'

'I don't like it,' said Petrus. 'Turn off.'

'Can't,' said Garrett. 'No turnings and if we stop and reverse, it'll look suspicious. Just be calm. I'm sure that it's nothing. We stop, tell them that we're tourists and go on our way.'

'Okay,' agreed Petrus. 'Let's do it.'

Garrett pulled to a stop at the traffic cone and wound his window down.

One of the soldiers walked over, his AK slung over his shoulder, his face a mask of indifference and boredom. Until he looked into the cab. Then he sprang back, almost tripping over his own feet, whipped his AK into a firing position and shouted.

'It's them. The white man and the Zulu.'

Two more soldiers sprinted over, one of them a captain, pointing their rifles. Another two stood in front of the jeeps, also holding their rifles ready.

'Get out,' shouted the captain. 'Hands above your heads and get out. Now!'

'Is this when we tell them that we're tourists?' asked Petrus under his breath.

'No,' said Garrett. 'This is where we get rid of them and get the hell out of Dodge.'

They both kicked open their doors at the same time, slamming them open as they jumped from the cab.

Garrett grabbed the soldier's rifle and pushed it up and away from him, at the same time shattering his knee with a front snap kick. Then he pulled the rifle back towards himself, dragging the soldier into a savage head butt that crushed his nose and knocked him instantly unconscious.

The captain pulled off a shot and the bullet whipped past Garrett. Close enough to pick at his hair. Garrett ripped his machete from its shoulder holster and swung hard. The razor-sharp blade connected with his assailant's forearm, biting deep. He dropped the rifle and Garrett snatched it up and clubbed him with the butt until he lay still.

He looked up to see Petrus standing above the prostrate body of the last soldier. The other two lay in pools of blood on the road. Petrus had simply stabbed them all with his assegai. Three savage blows. Three deaths.

'You had to kill them?' asked Garrett.

'We're not fishing here,' answered Petrus. 'This is not a catch and release hobby, *Isosha*. It's life or death. You know that.'

Garrett nodded. 'True. Let's move it. We need to find a place to lay low for a few hours. Can't go back to the hotel. The military and probably the cops, are looking for us.'

'What about the racecourse?' asked Petrus. 'We can hole up there until it's time to make our move on Chang.'

They got back into the pickup, did a U-turn and drove back to the racecourse, driving around it until they found a parking area that was hidden from the road.

They catnapped for a couple of hours and then Garrett retrieved their weapons from the concealed compartment and he started working on the C4 charges. He opened eight of the packs and worked them like dough, rolling and kneading until they softened enough to be able to form into shapes. He made three equal cone shaped charges. Into each charge he pushed a pencil detonator.

He passed two to Petrus. 'Here,' he said. 'You place one against Chang's back wall, then do the same with the other against the right-hand wall. I'll do the same with the left side and the front. The pencil timers are set for thirty minutes from now. Hopefully the charges should go off at around the same time, although that's not vital. After we've set them, we hotfoot it to that tree that we used earlier, climb up and fire a bazooka round at the top floor. Two if we reckon that we have time. Then we sprint back to the pick up and get the hell out. Agreed?'

Petrus nodded. 'Agreed.'

Garrett drove to the same point that they had parked before, close to Chang's house. Then they took their FN rifles, the charges and the superbazooka with two rounds. They took the bazooka to the mango tree that overlooked their target and lodged it in between two boughs about half way up.

After that they split up and went to place their explosives. Petrus went right, and Garrett left.

Chang's guards were placed inside the property, patrolling close to the walls. There were two outside the front gate and Garrett had spotted two on the roof who were constantly scanning the area.

Luckily there were no outside spotlights, so the sentries had to rely on the two working streetlights and the moon.

Moving unseen through the shadows is more of an art than a science. It does no good to simply attempt to hide or to merely stay out of sight. The odds are that you will, eventually, be spotted.

The secret is to become the shadows. And both Garrett and Petrus were masters of the art. They would move through the darkness, stopping when they were half in and half out. At the same time they would shape their bodies to blend with the lines of shade. Heads tilted to one side, an arm folded against their chest. A foot held a few inches above the ground so as to cast a small broken shadow. The object of the exercise was not to avoid being seen - it was to avoid the observer realizing what they were actually looking at, by using the light and shadow to create a false image. The phenomenon is called Scotoma - the mind sees what it chooses to see.

And some protagonists, like Garrett and Petrus, were so adept that it sometimes appeared that they had donned cloaks of invisibility.

Twenty minutes later they were climbing the tree and loading the superbazooka. At almost exactly the thirty-minute mark, the first charge exploded with a ground shaking thump. It was the one situated on the back wall and a cloud of dust rose high into the night sky.

There was instant pandemonium in the house. Lights went on, guards started to run from the building and shouts were heard from all points of the dwelling.

And then the next three charges detonated simultaneously. The right-hand wall was knocked down completely whilst the front and left wall had massive holes blasted through them. Two patrolling guards were caught in the left-hand blast and they were torn to shreds.

Then Petrus fired the bazooka. The rocket-propelled bomb flashed across the open space and hit the top left-hand window, smashing through the glass and detonating inside the room with a massive belch of flame.

Garrett quickly loaded another round into the tube and he patted Petrus on the shoulder.

'Ready.'

Petrus fired again. This round missed the window and exploded on the front of the building, smashing a gaping hole through it and covering the area with a wash of flame.

But the Flying Tigers were no normal group of troops. They were battle hardened and very well trained. Some of them had already assessed the situation and were firing back. The crack and snap of hypersonic steel rounds whipped past the two men as they shinned down the tree as quickly as they could.

Ducking low, they sprinted down the street away from the colonel and his troops.

They got to the pickup and piled in. Garrett drove, spinning the wheels as he accelerated away. They had studied the map book before and the plan was to head out of town and into the rural areas to lay low for a while. Then they would return, either on foot or with a stolen vehicle, and continue their campaign.

Already they could hear a multitude of sirens echoing around. In a town where police response was, at best patchy, it appeared that they were taking this occurrence seriously.

'Too many cops,' said Petrus. 'They were waiting for something to happen.' He pointed down the road. 'More cops. Take a turn.'

Garrett dragged the wheel to the right and they skidded around the corner. He cut the lights at the same time in an attempt to help concealment. Up ahead there were more police cars as well as two army jeeps. He went left.

He had no idea where he was as this was totally off their planned escape route but he reckoned that he was heading in the correct general direction, so he kept his foot down hard. A line of police and army vehicles snaked behind him. A metal conga line.

He turned another corner. A hundred yards in front was a roadblock. Two cars across the road and a police motorbike parked in front of them. Behind the cars stood policemen with sidearms drawn.

There was no warning. No due process. They simply opened fire on the pickup. Fortunately, they appeared to be the worst shots in the world as not one slug came close.

Garrett hit the brakes.

'I've had enough of this shit,' said Petrus. He grabbed the superbazooka, jumped out of the cab and ran around to the back, facing the oncoming conga of government vehicles. He rammed a round in and raised it to his shoulder, taking aim.

'Petrus. No!' shouted Garrett. But he was too late.

Petrus pulled the trigger.

The M20 superbazooka launches a nine-pound high explosive rocket up to a distance of one thousand yards. This creates a significant back blast that will severely damage anything within twenty-five meters of the back of the tube. In fact, there are several recorded cases of bystanders being killed by the said blast. When firing from the tree as they had earlier that evening, the back blast simply dissipated through the leaves and into the open air behind.

However, now Petrus was standing with the pickup directly behind him. The burst of flame hammered into the vehicle, smashing all of the windows and rocking it back on its suspension. Garrett was thrown to the ground and his dustcoat caught alight. He rolled frantically to extinguish the flames.

The rocket streaked through the air and hit the second car in the conga line, exploding in a massive ball of flame. Molten shards of metal punched through the cars in front of and behind the target, igniting their fuel tanks and causing a series of secondary explosions.

Petrus glanced behind him and his jaw dropped open.

'What the…?'

'Back blast,' yelled Garrett. 'You almost killed your partner in crime.'

'Sorry,' apologized the Zulu. 'I had no idea.'

'No worries. Let's get back in the pick up and get through this roadblock.'

Petrus threw the bazooka into the load area and jumped into the driver's seat. The policemen at the roadblock were still shooting at them, and it seemed that the practice was improving their aim. Bullets were ricocheting off the tarmac around them. Too close for comfort.

The pickup leapt forward. Garrett stuck the barrel of his FN out of the windscreen-less cab, lined up with the roadblock, flicked the fire-selector rate to fully automatic and pulled the trigger, sweeping the barrel from left to right. The windows of the police cars disintegrated and bright star shaped scars appeared in the doors and fenders as the 7.62mm rounds poured out at a rate of twelve per second.

The magazine ran dry as the pickup hit the motorbike, slamming it aside as it did so. Petrus aimed at the small gap between the two cars and struck it perfectly, spinning them both out of the way as he powered through.

The pickup barreled on through the night, heading west, through Kuwadzana and Dzivarasekwa and on towards the rural area around Lake Chivero.

Eventually it was swallowed up by the night.

CHAPTER TWENTY-EIGHT

Chinese ambassador mister Lin Chun and senior colonel Zhao Yuan stared at Jin Chang, both of their faces a portrait of scorn and disgust.

'*Ren hou lian, shu hou pi*,' said the ambassador to Chang. 'Men can't live without face, just as trees can't live without bark.'

Chang looked down. His demeanor that of a scolded child.

'You have brought shame to yourself, your embassy and your country. We have always looked the other way when it came to your transgressions,' continued Lin Chun.

Chang looked up. 'Of course you did,' he snapped. 'I paid you enough to do so. But now, in my hour of need, you abandon me.'

'Silence,' roared the ambassador. 'How dare you speak back to me. You have no face. You are worthless. Now, you still have your Flying Tigers. I want you to take them and use them to clear up this mess before we have an international incident. The only reason that I am not sanctioning you completely, is that misses Mugabe has personally spoken up for you.'

'Five of my Tigers are dead,' said Chang. His voice sulky.

'That is not our problem,' interjected senior colonel Zhao Yuan. 'You still have twenty-five of the world's best elite soldiers. Misses Mugabe has promised the full backing of both the police and the Fifth Brigade. The fact that she felt that she had to do this has, in itself, resulted in yet another loss of face for our government. Sort this problem out, colonel Chang, and do it soon.'

'Now leave us,' commanded the ambassador.

Chang stood, bowed and left the room. Sergeant Feng was waiting for him outside the ambassador's office.

'Come,' commended Chang. 'We have work to do.'

***

The colonel had hired the entire Southern Cross guest lodge. The owner had been understandably concerned, not usually catering for a Chinese army colonel and an entire team of special force troops.

But a carrot, in the form of a large wad of cash, delivered with a certain amount of stick, in the form of a loaded and cocked pistol, turned his frown upside down.

Sergeant Feng had the Flying Tigers on a constant guard rota, the police had put out an APB and the Fifth Brigade were on full alert and hunting for his attackers.

But still Chang felt uneasy. The attack on his house had been efficient, professional and a total surprise. The assailants had gotten away but his special forces had managed to get a fleeting glimpse of them. Two men, one black and one white. There could be no mistaking the fact that it was the Zulu and the white man that Roddy had spoken of. It was also patently obvious that these were very dangerous, heavily armed men.

They were out to get him and he had no idea why, which made the entire situation all the more frightening.

The colonel was under no illusions - the sun had truly set on his time in Zimbabwe. Now was the appropriate moment to move on. He would start again. Build a new empire. He had the money, the men and the contacts. Africa was his feeding ground. The people were his cattle.

'Feng,' he said. 'Tomorrow, I want you to take four of the men and go to the central bank. You will meet with mister Mikize. Here is a key. He will take you to a safe deposit box. There is a suitcase in it. Bring it to me. Then, we shall play the waiting game.'

arrett and Petrus had driven west, leaving the main roads at first and then eschewing even the dirt roads that followed. They crawled slowly into the virgin bush and, after a couple of hours, they stopped. The two of them hacked down some branches from the surrounding thorn trees, camouflaged the pickup and then crept under it to get some sleep.

They woke with the sun, ate some dry trail biscuits and drank some water.

'We need to stay here for a short while,' said Garrett. 'Maybe a couple of days or so. Looks like every man and his dog are looking for us. Bloody army, police. If they had a navy, I'm sure that they would be patrolling for us as well.'

'This Chang must be pretty well connected,' said Petrus. 'Someone high up has unleashed the dogs on us. What do you reckon that we do next?'

'I suggest that we lay low, don't move. After that we go back into Harare, track this Chang down again and make life seriously uncomfortable for him.'

Petrus nodded.

Later that afternoon a Cessna 206 single engine spotter plane over flew them. It didn't stop or slow down but it did turn after a while and continue its search above the area.

'Shit,' said Garrett. 'They know that we're here.'

'Maybe not,' argued Petrus. 'Could just be a general search.'

'Can't take the chance,' said Garrett. 'I reckon that we should move.'

Petrus agreed and they started the pickup and bumped further away from any major civilization. But there were still people, albeit small quantities of them. Herd boys, hunters, wood collectors and simple travelers. Both Garrett and Petrus kept their eyes open and, if they saw someone, they stopped to lay low.

Just before night they looked back at their last camp to see a helicopter hovering above it, machine gun poking out of the side door. It did a grid search of the immediate area and then flew off.

They grinned with relief and dug in for the night, using grass and branches to camouflage their meager campsite.

***

Bongani whistled as he walked with his herd of goats. There were eight of them. Short, wiry animals with sharp yellow teeth and a look of dull malevolence about them. There was a day when any self-respecting Matabele would not have been seen dead herding such a lowly animal. Bongani's father talked of times when they had owned a herd of twelve cows. Majestic animals that proved a man's worth and gave him stature in society.

Now they had goats. And goats were not good. They ripped the roots of the grass up when they grazed. Destroying it like spoiled children with no thought of tomorrow. Leaving a path of destruction wherever they went.

Not like cattle. A cow would crop the tips of the grass, promoting growth and eating its fill at the same time. But there were no more cattle. There was no more anything anymore. The white farmers had all gone so there was no work. And the land that Mugabe had appropriated had been left to go fallow. So, Bongani supposed, it didn't actually matter that the goats destroyed the land, there was no other use for it and there was plenty to go around.

And having eight goats was far better than having nothing at all.

Bongani, stopped whistling and took out his sling. A simple piece of leather with two pieces of string attached. He loaded a small stone, whirled and let fly.

It was a perfect strike, hitting the small mossie sparrow and killing it instantly. The little hunter picked up the bird and added it to the other five in his pouch. Later that day he would cook them, burning the feathers off over an open fire and then eating the rest whole, intestines and all.

He kept his eyes wide open for bigger birds. It would please his father greatly if he brought home something substantial to eat. It was difficult for his father to obtain food ever since he had stood on old anti-personnel mine left over from the war. Bongani had been with him when it had happened. A small crack. A puff of dust and smoke. And his father no longer had a left leg below his knee.

Now he had two sticks to help him walk, so he moved very slowly. Like a chameleon.

Bongani saw a small movement up ahead. He pulled his sling out again and moved forward in a low crouch. He peered through the grass.

And then he saw him. A white man sitting next to a truck. His heart leapt in excitement. That very morning, some soldiers had come to his village and told of a white man and a black man traveling together in the area. Any information would be richly rewarded, they had said.

Bongani crept silently away. His father would be more pleased with this than even a large bird. This would provide dollars. Perhaps even enough to buy a month worth of food.

And then he felt a huge hand grab him by the shoulder.

Petrus dragged the young herd boy into the camp and sat him down next to their tiny smokeless fire.

'Look what I found, spying on us,' he said to Garrett. 'I heard the goats so I went to take a look. This little bugger was doing a bit of a recce so I picked him up.'

The boy did not move from where Petrus had sat him down. His eyes were wide open in terror and his lips quivered.

The two men stared at him for a while.

Eventually Garrett spoke. 'Shit,' he said.

'And then some,' agreed Petrus. 'The moment he gets home he's going to tell all, and then it's only a matter of time before they're onto us. They've probably already offered a reward for info on us, after all, they suspect that we're in the general vicinity.'

'We can't tie him up,' said Garrett. 'We can't take him with us.'

'Could kill him,' suggested Petrus.

Garrett looked blankly at him. 'Don't even joke.'

'Okay, just throwing ideas out there. Use them, don't use them. Whatever.'

'I won't tell,' said Bongani in a shaking voice.

'Course you will,' said Petrus.

'I won't.'

'Shut up, boy,' snapped the Zulu.

Garrett took out a box of cigarettes, lit two and passed one to Petrus. Bongani stared at the cigarettes. Garrett offered him.

'Here, boy. You want one?'

Bongani nodded and took one from the pack. Then he slipped it behind his ear.

'For my father,' he explained.

Garrett threw him the rest of the pack. 'Here. For you father. Now fuck off. Quickly before I change my mind.'

Bongani sprang to his feet, a broad smile across his face. 'Thank you, sir,' he said. 'I won't tell. I promise.'

'Yes, you will,' disagreed Petrus.

The young herd boy sprinted off, whistling for his goats as he did so.

'Who knows?' said Garrett. 'Maybe he won't tell.'

'Bullshit,' said Petrus. 'We had better break and get moving. Place will be crawling with uglies soon.'

Garrett laughed. 'Have some faith in human nature, my friend. A bit of trust never goes amiss.'

They set off again, creeping slowly into the interior. Late that afternoon they looked back and saw three light airplanes grid searching the area where they had seen Bongani.

'Ha, told you,' exclaimed Petrus. 'He sold us out.'

Garrett said nothing.

That night they stopped and, once again, camou-flaged up.

They couldn't risk a fire so they simply sat in the dark and smoked in silence. Eventually Garrett spoke.

'We need to talk, my friend,' he said. 'Things are not going according to plan. We're pretty much stuck out here in the wilderness for the foreseeable future. Soon we're going to need more gas, food, water. Seems like the entire country is looking to do us harm. Tactically…well…I'd say that we are pretty close to fucked.'

Petrus shrugged. 'I've been in better situations,' he admitted.

'Look,' continued Garrett. 'What I wanted to say is - maybe we've done enough. We've killed the people directly responsible for Malusi's death and we've scared the crap out of the next in the chain. To all intents and purposes, we have screwed up their business. Retribution has taken place. If we continue this way…I can't see things ending well for us.'

'It is not enough,' said Petrus.

Garrett nodded. 'Okay. When will it be enough? The colonel? His soldiers? The man who controls the colonel? And what about his people? His family, friends? The people that owe him money? When will it end?'

'I do not know,' answered Petrus. 'Malusi will tell me. He will give me a sign.'

'What sign?'

'I will know it when I see it,' said Petrus, his voice full of confidence.

'Okay then,' said Garrett. 'Then we had better get some sleep because we need to get back to Harare and find this colonel.'

Petrus smiled. 'Thank you, my friend.'

The next morning, they woke, took out the map and plotted a course back to Harare. Before they got going another light aircraft flew over. Then it did a slow turn and waggled its wings when it flew above them again.

'Shit,' exclaimed Garrett. 'We've been spotted.'

'Nothing that we can do about it,' said Petrus. 'Let's get going.'

They saddled up and set off.

The sun hammered down on them, the heat a physical presence that leached the moisture from them, drying their eyes and their throats. After a couple of hours, they had to stop the pickup in order to let the engine cool down. They raised the hood to help the air to circulate and waited.

Garrett heard the sound first. Far away. Just on the very edge of hearing.

'Listen,' he said to Petrus. 'Engine. Maybe two.'

Petrus cocked his head to one side. 'Yes,' he agreed. 'Trucks. Two of them.'

They slammed the hood down and set off once more, trundling through the African veld.

Soon they came across a stretch of land covered by fist-sized rocks, strewn thick as far as the eye could see. Garrett changed down to first and they crunched across, steering around the bigger boulders. The pick up slid and swayed as the wheels spun and juddered over the treacherous rockscape.

There was a sudden bang as the front right tire sank into a hidden hole, slamming the bottom of the vehicle onto the rocks. Immediately a smell of diesel pervaded the cab.

'Shit,' cursed Garrett. 'We've holed the gas tank.'

The two of them sprung from the cab, gabbed the jack and feverishly cranked the vehicle up. Garrett slid underneath and checked.

'Yep,' he said. 'Hole as big as my thumb. Have you got any soap?'

'Sure,' replied Petrus. 'Also, toothpaste and shaving cream. Why don't you have quick shave while you're down there?'

'Fuck off,' retorted Garrett. 'Just get me a bar of soap. I'm sure that there's one in the washbag with the medic kit. Hurry, I can't lie here all day with my finger stuck in a gas tank, people will talk.'

Petrus rooted around in their packs and came back with a bar of soap. He handed it to Garrett. The soldier broke it in half and then rubbed some diesel onto it, working it in his hands as he did so. In a few seconds it had converted into a putty-like consistency. He forced it into the hole and smeared the excess around the hole, plugging it tight. Then he slid out, wiping his hands on his trousers as he did so.

'Clever,' admitted Petrus.

'Yep,' said Garrett. 'But we lost most of our fuel. We better get moving.'

The sound of the approaching engines was closer now. Much closer.

They cleared the rock-strewn area and ploughed on. After another hour the sun began to set and, at the same time, the engine coughed and spluttered. And died.

'That's that,' said Garrett. 'Shank's pony from now on. But first, let's rig a few surprises for whoever is following us.'

Garrett rigged the pick up's doors with claymores and then pulled the pins almost completely from two grenades and dropped them into the cab. Then they loaded up their packs, food, water, medical kit, C4 explosive, extra ammunition, the Bren gun and the superbazooka, claymores and grenades.

They set off at right angles to the direction that they had been going and they covered their tracks as best they could, hoping to avoid being followed. They walked for an hour but there was no moon and the going was slow and dangerous so they stopped and slept.

The two of them woke before the sun and set off immediately, walking fast. After ten minutes they heard the ragged thumps of the claymores and the grenades exploding as their pursuers set off the booby traps.

Garrett grinned. 'Take that,' he murmured under his breath.

A few minutes later they heard the engines start up again.

They started to run. Moving at a soldier's pace. Each carrying almost one hundred pounds of kit. Long loping strides that ate up the earth and used minimal energy. All day they ran, not pausing once. Drinking on the move, taking the route that they considered hardest for the trucks to follow.

And they stayed ahead.

Barely.

When the sun began to sink back into the nether-world, they finally stopped to take a breather. They were both utterly exhausted. But the enemy was so close now that they could actually smell the vehicles diesel fumes when the wind blew in the right direction.

Petrus drank deeply from his water canteen 'You know, Isosha,' he said. 'I think that it's time that we went on the offensive. I can't speak for you but I don't think that I can keep this up for another whole day.'

'Well, they do say that the best form of defense is to attack,' agreed Garrett.

'Personally, I've always found the best form of defense to be a good defense,' said Petrus. 'Whatever, I'm going to do a quick recce. You wait here. If I don't come back, you can have my watch.'

'You don't have a watch.'

Petrus grinned, his teeth shining white in the moon-less night. 'True.' He disappeared, like a ghost, into the darkness.

Twenty minutes later he returned.

'It's the Chinese,' he whispered. 'Two ACP's. Twenty soldiers. They don't appear to have heavy weapons. Three sets of guards. They're patrolling in pairs. They randomly change their routes, they stay alert, they don't smoke. They're good. Well disci-plined.'

'Could we take the guards out?' Asked Garrett.

Petrus shrugged. 'One set, easy. Two, maybe. Three, no way. Not without the alarm being given. I told you, these guys are good.'

Garrett thought for a while.

'Right,' he said. 'I've got a plan.'

Chang had moved from the guesthouse when the bulk of his troops had gone on hot pursuit of his two attackers. He had hired out the Imperial suite at Miekles hotel in Harare. To ensure his privacy he had also hired out the presidential suite and all of the rooms on the floor below. It was costing him in excess of twenty thousand dollars a night.

He had retained four Flying Tigers and they were staying in the corridor outside his room. Cots had been set up so that two could sleep while two stood guard. Sergeant Feng slept in the room next to his. He was taking no chances.

But he had just received good news. Corporal Yeung had just radioed in. They were hard on the trail of the two fugitives and were confident of overhauling them the next day. The corporal did not mention the booby-trapped pick up. Nor the loss of three of his men. He knew that this small failure would be forgiven when he brought the colonel the heads of the renegades.

Colonel Chang sat in front of an octagonal marble topped table that graced the center of the sitting area of the room. On the table sat a large leather suitcase. It was open. Inside were neat bundles of one-hundred-dollar bills.

The suitcase was made by Hermes and was worth a staggering eight thousand dollars. The contents added another twenty-two million to that total.

'Sergeant Feng,' called Chang. 'Come through.'

The sergeant walked through from his room and stood in front of the colonel. 'Sir?'

'Sergeant, I have decided on our future. This morning I booked a train. A locomotive and two carriages for our private use. We will travel from here to Bulawayo and then onwards to Lusaka in Zambia. From there we will proceed on to Dar Es Salaam. I have always wanted a place overlooking the sea. We will live like kings.'

'Yes, sir,' agreed Feng. 'You will.'

'What?'

'Nothing, sir,' replied the sergeant. 'Simply agreeing.'

'Good. We will take the four Tigers here and I want you to contact corporal Yeung. Tell him the plan. Tell him that I have decided to rebuild in Dar Es Salaam. All are welcome as soon as they have dealt with the two renegades. Their pay will be doubled. They will have to decide whether to stay with the people's army or become part of their own thing. If they want to be a part of the new empire that I shall build tell Yeung to proceed to Bulawayo as soon as he has completed his mission. Sell them all on the idea, sergeant. I foresee great things for us.'

Feng nodded. As he walked off, he thought again of his sister. And the mountains. And his parents who could not read or write. The family that he had not seen or spoken to for over six years. He remembered an old Chinese proverb; Life is a dream walking; death is a going home. And he finally admitted to himself, he would never go home. This afternoon he would wire all of his savings to his parents. Then he would follow the colonel into whatever suicidal delusion he had waiting for them. Because the sergeant was not cursed with Chang's psychotic level of naïve megalomania and he knew that, if you stole an entire detachment of Special Forces from the Chinese government, they would hunt you down for the rest of eternity. But he no longer cared.

He switched the radio on and contacted corporal Yeung.

CHAPTER THIRTY-ONE

Garrett and Petrus used the cover of the moon free night to plant the Mk5 land mine in the middle of their tracks. They dug in from the side of the trail rather than digging directly down so as to conceal the point of ingress. No tell-tail mound of earth to give the explosives position away. Then he placed four of the claymores around the side of the track. They were there to catch the soldiers who jumped from the stricken vehicle or those who came to help.

Then the two of them went one hundred and fifty yards down the track and Garrett used the remaining claymores to create a choke point, stringing two on each side, not bothering to conceal the steel trip wires. They were there to funnel the enemy together, more than to surprise them. At the bottom of the channel that he had formed he dug a shallow trench, built a small parapet and lay the Bren gun on top, the spare magazines in a row next to it. By the time he had finished the sun was threatening to rise and a false dawn had washed the darkling sky with a haze of gray.

'Right,' he said to Petrus. 'I need you to get behind them. Skirt around the right flank and then get in close. When the first APC hits the mine they will probably take casualties. Anyone who runs from the APC, or anyone who dismounts the second vehicle and goes to help will detonate the claymores. That's when I'll hit them from the front using my FN. I'll make sure that I am exposed and then I'll leg it down the track. They should pursue me, but they're good, so I am sure that they will do so with caution. I fully expect them to spot the next block of claymores but that doesn't matter, I'll be taking pot shots at them to keep them from thinking too hard. As they funnel themselves into the killing ground I want you to open up with the superbazooka. I will lay down fire with the Bren at the same time. We hit them hard and fast and then split before they can regroup. Remember, Petrus, I cannot stress how good these guys are. Don't take any chances. When it's over, we meet at the foot of the koppie with the three thorn trees.'

Petrus nodded. 'Got it. Let's party.'

Garrett knew that every battle plan would only last until the first shot is fired. From that moment on it rapidly degenerates into more of a rough guideline coupled with a frantic prayer session.

So, as far as battle plans went, this one did not go so badly - to a point.

The leading APC struck the mine with a resultant boom of fire and dust. The troops poured out of the damaged vehicle and three of them ran directly into the claymores detonating a storm of steel balls that scythed them down in a welter of flesh and blood.

Garrett opened up on them, picking his targets by the light of the rising sun. The return fire was unbelievable. All around him the air turned to fire. The bullwhip crack of supersonic copper jacketed steel assaulted his ears and the close passage of superheated air buffeted him from side to side as they missed him by mere thousands of an inch.

'Shit,' said Garrett to himself. 'These guys are good.'

He pulled off a few more rounds and then ran, zigzagging from side to side as he did so. The ground exploded all about him and small boughs and leaves rained down from the trees as the sheer weight of fire decimated all in his immediate area. Something hit him hard in his left calf, kicking his leg out from under him and sending him rolling to the ground. He tried to get up but his leg collapsed and he fell again. Desperately he ripped a grenade from his webbing, pulled the pin and threw it. Immediately he followed it with another. The rate of incoming fire stuttered and slowed for a few seconds.

Garrett used the slight lull to raise himself up and stagger away, pushing himself as hard as he could. He could feel his boot filling with blood. Warm. Sticky.

Sweat ran into his eyes, obscuring his vision. His swiped it away with the back of his hand. He searched frantically for the claymores. Squinting to see the trip wires. Finally, he saw them, picked out by the sun like a morning spider web covered in dew. He headed down the funnel, throwing himself into his shallow trench, fervently hoping that it would not become a shallow grave.

Then the ground shook with the deep savage detonation of the superbazooka round. A cloud of fire rolled skyward and the surrounding trees burst into flame. Garrett peered down the barrel of the Bren and opened up. A man went down.

Petrus fired from behind.

The Bren ate the magazines of ammo up. The beats shouted out in joy as the battle madness overcame Garrett. Fire. Fire. Change magazine. Throw grenade. Fire again.

He could no longer hear the deep thud of the FN that is easily discernable from the high crack of the Chinese 5.8x42mm rounds.

Garrett looked for Petrus. Why couldn't he hear his rifle firing? Has he been hit? No. He's on the move. Calm down. Think. Garrett crawled for the trench and then stood up and ran, moving with inherent stealth. Becoming part of the bush. More animal than human.

Blood, sweat, cordite.

The green smell of raw sap from the splintered trees. The gritty taste of dust mixed with salty sweat.

Garrett fell again, rolling as he hit the ground. He pulled his bootlaces as tight as he could. Then he tore a sleeve off his shirt and tied it around his calf, pulling it taut until the bleeding stopped.

He got to his feet and ran on.

He met Petrus at the foot of the hill. The Zulu squatted under a tree. He had a bloody bandage wrapped around his head like a sweatband. The blood had soaked through and both of his shoulders were wet with red.

'Hey, *Isosha*,' he greeted. 'I keep getting shot in the head. I'm worried that my brains are going to fall out.'

'What brains?' gasped Garrett as he lay down, panting.

'I could have bet you would have said that,' said Petrus. 'Now let me see what I can do for your leg. It doesn't look good and we don't have much time.' He leant over Garrett and used a knife to cut his trouser leg away. Then he pulled Garrett's makeshift dressing off to expose the wound.

'It's not a bullet wound,' he said. 'Looks like a piece of shrapnel, a sliver of stone or something. It's cut you deep.' He dug through his pack, pulled out the medical kit, opened it and selected some surgical thread and a curved needle. 'I'll stitch it quickly,' he continued. 'No need to clean it, the flow of blood will have done that already. He threaded the needle, pinched the lips of the wound together and inserted six rough stitches and bound it again. 'There. Good as new. Now let's go.'

He put the medic kit back and shouldered his webbing as he stood up.

Garrett followed suit, grimacing at the pain. 'You're right, we gotta keep moving, stay ahead of them. Then come nightfall, we hit them again. Finish the job.'

The two friends had stayed ahead of the Flying Tigers all day. They had used the landscape, cutting across broken land as much as they could to force the Chinese to disembark and split up, some on foot whilst the APC had to drive around the broken land and rocks and rendezvousing with them afterwards.

Petrus and Garrett had killed ten Tigers and badly wounded two others in the ambush. But they were exhausted. Fatigued almost unto the very door of death itself.

In fact, both of them had started to hallucinate.

Petrus talked to his brother, Malusi as he ran. Smiling and nodding.

Garrett could hear the cries of children. He could hear their screams of agony. And all about him the landscape shimmered and changed. Vacillating between the desiccated brown of Zimbabwe to the verdant green of Sierra Leone. Wraiths danced ahead of him, crooking their fingers at him. Calling him.

Then the beast howled and drove them all away, bringing Garrett back to reality. He ran next to Petrus and shook him, dragging him back to the present, forcing him to stay sharp. Focused.

They paused an hour after mid-day to snatch something to eat and drink, but Petrus fell asleep instantly and Garrett had to slap him repeatedly to awaken him.

Eventually night fell and, as soon as the darkness enfolded them. Petrus fell to the floor and instantly slept. Garrett kept watch for as long as he could, almost two hours, then he woke Petrus and asked him to keep watch while he snatched two hours sleep.

Almost exactly two hours later Petrus woke him. It was still as dark as pitch.

Garrett mixed some water and sand and used the mud to darken his face. Then they both smeared the mud on their blades to avoid any reflection. They set off together, leaving their firearms but carrying two hand grenades each.

And they became children of the night, questing out to slake their thirst. Shades amongst the shadow. Lions seeking the blood of man.

There were four sentries on guard, leaving the other four survivors asleep next to their campfire.

Together, Garrett and Petrus moved in on the first sentry. A young man, alert. His eyes scanning constantly, letting the rods in his peripheral vision pick up any night time movement. And then the shadow in the valley of death came alive and took him. The only sound, the silken whisper of steel slicing through human flesh followed by the almost imperceptible patter of blood on earth.

The shadow moved on.

Three more sentries died in absolute silence. They were there - then they were not.

Still moving with a stealth necessitating slowness, Garrett and Petrus took out two grenades each, pulled the pins and lobbed them next to the fire. Four vicious cracks and four blinding flashes rent the night.

Garrett and Petrus closed their eyes and blocked their ears so they suffered no disorientation and, as soon as the grenades had exploded, they ran in. The four people next to the fire were all dead. The two friends checked, looking for colonel Chang, but the men were all enlisted troops. No colonel. They ran to the APC and looked inside. There were two wounded men, wrapped in their sleeping bags. Both too badly injured to react.

'Shit,' shouted Garrett. 'No colonel.' He grabbed one of the wounded men and shook him. 'Where is the colonel?'

The man looked blankly at him, his eyes wide with delirium.

Petrus leant in close, using wile instead of the threat of violence. 'The colonel. We need him. Please, help us.'

The young soldier stared at the Zulu for a while. Then he spoke in the slightest whisper. 'Corporal Yeung said that colonel Chang is going to Dar Es

Salaam,' he said. 'He has taken a private train, two coaches and an engine. He is taking us all from Bulawayo to Lusaka and then to Dar Es Salaam. We will all be Yi Deng Bo or chief of the first rank.' He grasped Petrus' sleeve. 'Pain,' he gasped. 'So much pain.'

Garrett searched the APC, going through the various cubbyholes. Eventually he pulled out a metal case. Gray with a red cross on. He opened it.

'This looks like morphine,' he said, holding up a syrette.

Petrus shrugged. 'Maybe.'

Garrett moved over to the young Tiger, rolled his sleeve up and injected him. Within seconds the drug took effect and the young man relaxed.

'We need to get to get to that train. Preferably before it gets into Zambia,' said Petrus. 'Best to catch it between Bulawayo and the border if we can.'

'We'll take the APC,' said Garrett.

'What about these two?' Asked Petrus, gesturing to the pair of wounded Flying Tigers.

'There're pretty fucked,' said Garrett. 'Surprised that they're still alive. Tough bastards both of them. I reckon that we pump them full of morphine, leave them by the fire. Harsh, but we did shoot both of them in the first place as they were trying to kill us at the time.'

'You'll find no arguments here,' agreed Petrus.

Twenty minutes later, after drugging the wounded Tigers and collecting all of the weapons and ammo, the two friends were heading towards Bulawayo, cutting cross-country with the APC.

CHAPTER THIRTY-THREE

Late the next morning they drove into a small village. After contacting the headman, they purchased an old Toyota pickup, paying for it with the APC and a handful of dollars. They also left the headman the FN rifles, some of the surplus Chinese rifles and a hundred rounds of ammunition. They took three rifles and the rest of the ammunition with them.

The pick up's odometer stated that the vehicle had traveled seventy-two miles. Which meant that it had gone around the clock at least once, if not twice. A mileage somewhere between one hundred and two hundred thousand. Halfway to the moon. It was predominantly white in color apart from the two doors, one green and one a faded yellow. A row of bullet holes was stitched down the right hand side of the loading bay.

But it worked, spluttering along in a cloud of smoke like an old-fashioned steam train.

Every few hours they would see another spotter plane in the sky above them, but they were confident of not being seen as the battered old pick up provided a great disguise.

'Someone high up in government has a real hard on for us,' said Petrus. 'They're still searching for us. This Chang asshole must be personal friends with Mugabe or someone.'

'Yeah,' agreed Garrett. 'Who would have known? Just our luck.'

As Petrus drove he would randomly comment on things. A sighting of an animal. A request for a cigarette. A particular type of tree. An attempt to break the monotony.

But Garrett remained silent. The Beast had been driven back into its cage. Bound tight with bonds of steel and willpower. And its absence had left a deep pool of regret. Once again, he was in Africa. Once again, he was killing. And for what? Some outdated concept of ancestor worship? A mere sop to a friend's grief and desire for revenge.

He knew that Petrus was killing for something that he believed in. He was killing to save his brother's soul. He believed that he was doing something that had to be done to ensure his brother's everlasting peace. He was killing out of love.

But Garrett feared that he was killing merely to satisfy the Beast. Feeding it with the souls of the innocent.

'They were bad men,' said Petrus.

'What?' Asked Garrett, drawn out of his internal reverie by Petrus' seeming non-sequitur.

'Those soldiers. The Chinese. They worked for a man who ran protection rackets. A man who bullied and ordered killings. Forced people into prostitution and drug dealing. A man who is partly responsible for destroying almost an entire species of animal. A man who is partly responsible for my brother's death. And they are part of this man.'

'They were just soldiers,' said Garrett.

'True,' agreed Petrus. 'But would you take orders to do the things that they did?'

Garrett shook his head. 'No.'

'You see,' said Petrus. 'They were bad men.'

Another spotter plane flew over them.

'Petrus looked up. 'They're still looking for us,' he said.

Garrett stared at it. 'No,' he said. 'That's the fourth time that we've been overflown. They're not grid searching, they're not changing direction. They simply fly over, straight and level and then disappear into the distance. They're trying not to attract too much attention. That's because they are no longer looking - they've already found us and they're simply keeping us under surveillance. We need to find some high ground so that we can check for someone following us.'

An hour later they came across a small koppie. Petrus parked at the bottom of it and the two of them jogged to the peak. Then Garrett took out his binoculars and scanned the surrounding vista. He stood for ages, not moving, simply scoping out the direction from whence they had just come.

He handed the binoculars to Petrus. 'There, maybe five clicks away, southwest. Some sort of APC.'

Petrus adjusted the focus. 'Got them. Coming fast.' The Zulu carried on watching for another full ten minutes. 'They're definitely following us. Right on our trail. Let's go.'

They ran down the hill and jumped into the pickup. Petrus revved the engine, smoke bellowed, valves clattered and the vehicle ground forward, surging through the virgin bush.

They drove as fast as they could and, whenever they saw high ground, they would stop and check on their pursuers.

Petrus looked through the binoculars and drew a deep breath. 'I don't have a good feeling about this,' he said. 'They are getting closer by the minute. Looks like their ride is an upgraded Crocodile APC. Got an FN 7.62 machine gun on the roof. Carries up to fifteen troops. What have we got? A couple of grenades. Three claymores, these shitty Chinese rifles. I tell you, *Isosha*, this sucks.'

Garrett said nothing. There was nothing to say. Petrus was right, they were exhausted, under armed and about to face a clearly superior force.

'We'll lose them tonight,' he said. 'Same again. We ditch the pickup, booby trap it using the last of the claymores and the grenade. Hopefully that will slow them down a bit. Then we need to up our game, make sure that they can't track us. We've got enough cash to buy some more transport when we come across it. Let's move on out.'

They mounted up and continued driving. An hour before sunset they came across a dry riverbed. The course was covered with hundreds of large flat river rocks.

'This is it,' said Garrett. 'We leave the pick up here. Booby trap it and then move from rock to rock down the riverbed. There's no way that they'll be able to track us. We go as far as we can down the riverbed then we hotfoot it out of here, find some more transport and find the colonel. Kill him and then get the fuck out of this shitty country.'

'It's a plan,' said Petrus. 'Let's give it a go.'

Garrett laid the claymore traps carefully, connecting the tripwires to the door handles so that, as soon as someone tried to open the door, they would explode. Once again, he placed a grenade in the cab, its pin pulled almost out, to add to the destructive force of the explosion.

Then the two of them moved carefully to the riverbed, using bundles of grass to sweep their tracks. Once they were on the dry riverbed they moved from rock to rock. The going was very slow but they had decided to trade speed for concealment, determined to leave no discernable tracks.

When it was almost dark, they left the riverbed and walked for another hour. Then they stopped and slept, both so exhausted that they didn't even bother to keep watch, merely dropping to the floor and letting sleep overcome them.

Garrett woke the next morning before the sun and looked up to see Petrus standing still, staring out at the surrounding bush. 'What's the problem?' He asked. 'There's no way that they could be anywhere close. They can't have caught up with us and they have no idea where we are.'

'I just have this feeling,' said the Zulu. 'Like someone's watching us. Felt it last night as well.'

'It's nothing,' said Garrett. 'Let's eat and get going.'

Petrus pulled out some rations. Pronutro, a South African powdered food made from maize sugar, skim milk powder, groundnut flour, Soya flour, and fish protein concentrate with added vitamins. They mixed it with water. It had the consistency of quicksand and tasted like sawdust and sugar. But it was nutritious and energy giving, and that is why Petrus had packed it as their major food source.

As soon as they had eaten, they moved on to the first area of high ground that they could see.

Garrett scanned their trail with his binoculars, picking up their followers almost immediately, a few miles back, clustered around the old pick up.

The soldier held his hand up. 'They're all around the pickup,' he said. 'Won't be long.'

The two friends waited. But there was no explosion.

'They're not taking the bait,' said Garrett. 'Not even looking into the pick up, they're just scouting around the area. Looking for spoor. A lot of good that'll do them,' he continued. 'There's no way that they will be able to find our trail.' He was about to pack up his binoculars when he paused. 'No way,' he explained. 'They've picked it up. I can't believe it. How the fuck did they do that? Man, these guys are good.' He turned to Petrus. 'Let's go.'

And they ran. Long loping strides. They stopped for more Pronutro at midday and then continued running.

'Keep a look out for rocky ground,' said Garrett. 'Overhanging trees, anything that we think can throw them off the trail.'

Within an hour they came across an area of rock and shale. They entered the area and walked slowly across it, making sure that they didn't dislodge any rocks or leave any sort of trace of their passing. On the edge of the rocky plain there was a copse of large false Mopani trees. They grabbed one of the overhanging boughs and climbed up. Then they clambered from tree to tree across the copse before dropping to the ground.

'Yeah,' said Garrett. 'Try to track that, you fuckers.' He turned to Petrus. 'What do you reckon?'

But, once again, the Zulu was standing still, his head cocked to one side, listening.

'What?' asked Garrett.

Petrus shook his head. 'Nothing. Just spooked, I guess. Let's keep moving.'

The day became an endless, sunlit dust bowl; of pain and exhaustion. Bodies that had been pushed beyond collapse were pushed even further.

The deep cut in Garrett's leg felt like fire and Petrus' head wound thumped in time with every step that he took. In the last four days they had run almost two hundred miles, the equivalent of four standard marathons.

On top of that they had fought for two of the nights. They had been deprived of both sleep and sustenance and had now entered a stage where their bodies were actually eating themselves to provide enough fuel to continue their grueling pace.

They continued running into the night, staggering and lurching like zombies, until finally they simply fell down and lay there, comatose.

The next morning, before the sun, they were dragged from their death-like sleep by the sound of the following APC's diesel engine in the distance.

They stood up, stretched and ran again, looking for a high point. As soon as they found one, they climbed to the top of the hillock and surveyed the land.

Garrett watched them through the binoculars for a while. 'Well,' he said. 'Obviously they're still following us.'

'Man, these guys are good,' said Petrus.

'Better than me,' admitted Garrett. 'There is no way that I could have followed our tracks. Not with all that we did.'

Petrus took the binoculars and took a look. 'Shit,' he exclaimed. 'I know these fuckers.'

'What, personally?' asked Garrett.

'No, of course not. They're Fifth Brigade. You can tell by their red berets.'

'I've heard of them,' said Garrett. 'Aren't they some sort of fast reaction squad?'

'No,' denied Petrus. 'Not really. In nineteen eighty, president Mugabe signed an agreement with the North Korean President, Kim Il Sung, that they would train and equip a brigade for the Zimbabwe National Army. That turned out to be the Fifth Brigade. And they were different from all other army units. They were answerable only to the prime minister, and not to the normal army command structures. Mugabe basically used them as his own private death squad. In nineteen eighty-three, he sent them to crush any resistance, right here, in Matabeleland, because their leader was running against him. They slaughtered over twenty thousand civilians. Some say closer to fifty thousand. Most of the dead were shot in public executions, often after being forced to dig their own graves in front of family and fellow villagers. Others they simply burned alive in their huts.'

'How come you know so much about this?' asked Garrett.

'The Matabele are an Nguni tribe,' answered Petrus. 'Close relatives to the Zulu. My father knew many of them. They call that time of genocide, Gukurahundi.

This is most simply translated as "the rain that washes away the chaff before the spring rains." Trust me, *Isosha*, these are very bad fuckers. You don't want them to take you alive. The thing is,' mused Petrus. 'I have no idea why they are following us. We have no fight with them.'

'You said yourself that Chang must be well connected. Maybe even mates with Mugabe. I reckon that this sort of proves that theory. Whatever, it looks as though we've got a fight coming our way,' interjected Garrett. He looked around, taking in the hill and the approaches. 'This is as good a place as any,' he said. 'We will make our stand here.'

Petrus nodded. 'I am so sorry, my friend,' he said.

'Yeah, well. I always knew that this fucking continent would be my death. I always wanted to die in my bed. Old and infirm, surrounded by grandchildren and well-wishers. Only problem was, no kids and no grand kinds.'

'And no one who wished you well,' added Petrus.

They laughed together and started to build a rampart of stones on the crown of the hill. Then they placed all of their spare magazines on the rampart, sat down, smoked and drank the last of their water. There was no longer a need to conserve it.

They waited and twenty-five minutes later the APC trundled into view. Two trackers ran in front of it and an officer sat in the open top, behind the 7.62mm machine gun.

The officer shouted an order. Garrett and Petrus could not hear it above the engine but it was obvious what he was saying.

The APC stopped and the troops poured out. There were twelve of them. The machine gunner pointed at the hill, raised his arm and chopped it down. The APC crawled forward, the Fifth Brigade troops walking next to it, AKM assault rifles at the ready as they bore down on the hill.

'Well now,' said Garrett. 'Let's see how many of these fuckers we can take down.'

The two of them opened fire, concentrating on the officer in the cupola. Their shots ricocheted off the armor around him. Some slugs even struck close enough to flick at his clothing. But none hit him.

The return fire was absolutely overwhelming.

The machine gun opened up with a sound akin to a giant, tearing bales of cloth. The troops fired with their AKM's on full automatic at the same time. Each firearm was capable of churning out a cyclic rate of over ten rounds a second. Thirteen weapons firing at once tore the top of the hill to pieces. Fully two thousand rounds smashed into Garrett and Petrus' small redoubt in the first ten seconds. The thorn trees were leveled, the rampart simply ceased to exist and both Garrett and Petrus were hit.

Blood flowed and mixed with the dry dust forming a dull red mud. A quagmire of human DNA.

'I've been shot in the fucking head again,' said Petrus, blood pouring down a savage gash in his temple.

'Me too,' said Garrett wiping blood out of his eyes.

'Should we fire back?' Enquired the Zulu.

'Not sure,' answered Garrett. 'It'll just piss them off.'

'Oh well, fuck them,' said Petrus as he lined up his rifle again.

But before he could fire there was a flash of an explosion about fifty yards away from the APC. A trail of smoke connected the flash with the side of the APC. There was another muted bang as the projectile struck the side of the armored vehicle followed immediately by a massive secondary explosion.

The officer behind the machine gun was expelled from the vehicle in a gout of flame that threw him twenty yards into the air. His burning body hit the ground with a wet thump.

The Fifth Brigade troops turned to face the new threat but they didn't stand a chance. Another RPG rocket exploded amongst them and then a fusillade of small arms fire decimated their ranks. Steel jacketed bullets flying like swarming locusts of death as they fed upon the red bereted soldiers.

Garrett and Petrus joined in, firing as fast as they could and changing magazines with fervid haste.

'What the fuck is going on?' shouted Petrus.

'Not a clue,' answered Garrett. 'But they're shooting at the same people that we're shooting at, so don't complain.'

The firefight lasted another thirty seconds before it hiccupped to a halt. Garrett and Petrus heard some shouted orders. Indistinct due to the fact that their ears were ringing from the noise of the battle.

Amazingly, not all of the Fifth Brigade soldiers were dead, even though they had all been struck a number of times. However, their attackers were changing that fact, walking amongst the bodies and calmly shooting the survivors in the face.

'Who the hell are these guys?' asked Garrett.

Petrus shrugged. 'Don't know, but they have just become my official best friends. Unless they decide to shoot us next, then the friendship is over.'

'Let's go and talk,' suggested Garrett as he stood up, slinging his rifle over his shoulder. Petrus did the same and the two of them trudged down the hill.

The men that they were approaching were not dressed in uniform although their clothing was of a type. Mainly faded and patched denim with a motley selection of various types of webbing ranging from Vietnam era American to nineteen eighties South African. In the main they carried AK's also ranging from sixties model 47's to the more recent AKM.

The two friends headed towards a man who looked like he was probably in charge, by virtue of the fact that he was the one issuing the orders.

As they got closer, all of the men pointed their rifles at the two friends. The atmosphere was tense.

'The words, frying pan and fire come to mind,' said Garrett in a low voice. 'Not sure about you but I don't think that we're out of the shit yet.'

'Let me do the talking,' responded Petrus. 'Greetings,' he said to the leader. 'I am Petrus; this here is my friend Garrett. We are in your debt, stranger.'

The man nodded. 'My name is Mandla. These are my men. And you owe us nothing, friend,' he continued. 'Any opportunity to kill members of the Fifth Brigade are a welcome bonus to us.' He waved his hand at his men and they all lowered their rifles.

'I don't understand,' said Garrett. 'Who are you guys?'

'We are Matabele,' answered Mandla. 'Former members of ZIPRA, the Zimbabwe People's Liberation Army. We used to be part of the Patriotic Front and we fought alongside Mugabe and his Shona tribe during the war against the white oppressors. But after we won, Mugabe spurned us. He sent his Fifth Brigade monkeys to exterminate us. We killed many of them so he put a price on our heads. Now we live in seclusion, exiles in our own country. I myself used to be a major. A man of some substance. Now I am once again a simple guerilla fighter, living off the land.'

'But that was over twenty-five years ago,' said Garrett.

'Yes,' said Mandla. 'But hatred knows no time limits. The Fifth Brigade are our enemies. Now and always. And Mugabe has never rescinded his kill-on-sight order, nor will he. So, we are still at war. Even though twenty-five years have passed. Anyway, a few days ago we saw the Chinese come into our area so we followed them. We watched you kill them all and we thought that perhaps we should then kill you and take your weapons. But then the Fifth Brigade started to hunt you down - and so you became our brothers.'

'The enemy of my enemy is my friend,' commented Garrett.

'Yes,' declared Mandla. 'That is it exactly. So, we followed you and watched and waited for the right moment. The rest, you saw.'

'I knew that we were being followed by someone else,' said Petrus.

Mandla shook his head. 'No way, man. You suspected. You never knew for sure. We're good man. Real good. We've lived here our whole lives so we should be. Mind you, we were surprised that you even suspected. What did you see?'

Petrus shook his head. 'Nothing. I could feel someone's eyes on me, that's all.'

Mandla clicked his tongue in irritation. 'I've told my guys not to do that. Never look at someone too hard or too long, I told them. The good ones can feel that and you'll give away your position. So, let's get you guys stitched up, fed and watered and then you can tell us what the hell you are doing here. Then we will decide if we are all still friends.'

Mandla's men had already set up camp near to the destroyed APC after piling the dead bodies into a natural donga, a ditch, in the landscape and covering them with a screen of branches.

Mandla gestured for the two friends to sit next to the fire and an older man came and checked their wounds. A shard of steel had sliced Petrus' scalp open to the bone above his right ear. The old man introduced himself as Doc Johnston and he set about cleaning and stitching Petrus' lesion. He was very good, his stitches neat and the bandage tight and professional.

Garrett's wound was a little more problematic. He had actually been shot twice. Both glancing blows at almost right angles on the top of his head. A ragged X shaped gash. Doc Johnston tutted and shook his head as he worked, like the wound was Garrett's fault or that he had had a choice in the matter and had deliberately chosen a laceration that was difficult to stitch up.

But eventually Doc sorted it out. He wound a bandage around the soldier's head, taped it and gave him a thumb up in approval.

'I am sorry,' he said to both of them. 'I have nothing to give you for the pain. You will simply have to ignore it.'

Both Garrett and Petrus thanked him and complimented him on his work. He smiled, genuinely pleased.

Then Mandla called them to the cooking pot to help themselves to food.

The rebels had cooked a stiff maize meal porridge and, on the side, a gravy of onions, and Mopani worms, a worm that looked much like a silk worm, and a large amount of spicy hot curry powder. Both Garrett and Petrus ate until their stomachs felt distended, such was their need for sustenance.

'So,' said Mandla, once the two had eaten their fill. 'Tell me your story. Why are you here?'

So Petrus told their story, leaving nothing out. The rebels were all gathered round and they all showed much interest, asking questions if they needed clarification, voicing their displeasure when they felt the need and nodding their approval when they perceived a triumph.

At the end of the tale, they all clapped as if Petrus had just performed a play for their entertainment. Some patted him on the back and others chatted amongst themselves, condemning the villains and approving the heroes.

'Good story,' said Mandla. 'And well told. And the fact that the Fifth Brigade are after you means that you must have seriously annoyed that human turd, Mugabe. For that we are thankful. And I agree with you,' he addressed Petrus. 'You need to kill this Chinaman or your brother will not find rest. I think that I know someone who might help. Do you have money?'

Petrus nodded.

'Good. The man that you need is about six hours away. More if we walk. But before we go you two must rest. You both look as if death has already staked her claim on you and she is simply waiting for you to realize the fact.'

'I have felt better,' admitted Petrus.

The Doc came over with two threadbare gray blankets and handed one to each of them. 'Sleep,' he commanded. 'You are safe here. We will wake you when necessary.'

The two men lay down where they were, rolled themselves up in the blankets and fell immediately into a death like slumber.

CHAPTER THIRTY-FOUR

Mandla shook them both awake after eight hours. It was dark and the campfire had already been extinguished. He handed them a handful of cold maize cakes and a canteen of water. They ate and drank quickly, tightened their boots, put their webbing on, slung their rifles over their shoulders and stood ready.

Mandla led the way, heading northwest at a slow jog, keeping track by the light emitted by the sliver of a bright blue new moon. Garrett and Petrus ran behind him and behind them the rest of the rebels fanned out.

They ran without talk, their breathing low and steady. They stopped only for water and, after five hours, for a bite to eat. But no one complained or spoke out, they merely ran.

Garrett felt at ease. It had been a long time since he had last been in a large group of men such as these. Hard men. Men who fought for what they believed in. Men who lived off the land, never complained. Men who never even thought of death even though it was their constant companion. For they knew that any soldier that thinks of death would soon become a dead soldier. Because darkness is all encompassing and to contemplate it, is to allow it access. And then, instead of fighting, one instead attempts to avoid death. But there is no way that death can be avoided. It is inevitable. Implacable. So it was better to ignore it completely and, in doing so, to live one's life more completely.

Neither Garrett nor Petrus asked whom they were going to see or where they were going. To do so would have been disrespectful. Mandla had stated that he knew someone who might help and that was enough. To question him would be seen as the height of discourtesy.

So they simply ran on, keeping their eyes open, breathing easily. At one with their surroundings.

The sun rose in the African way. First the gray of the false dawn, then a retreat back into night and finally the sun itself, bold and red as it painted the land in shades of blood. They halted again for a quick food break and then continued.

Before the next hour was up, they got the first glimpse of what Garrett assumed must be their destination. A small, rectangular house, its roof a mix of corrugated iron and raw African thatch. A patio surrounded the house. Next to it an old windmill to draw water from the borehole. All around the dwelling were chickens and domesticated guinea fowl, running free. Also, dogs, three of them, all of such mixed parentage as to have homogenized into a breed that could only be described as Zimbabwean bush mongrel.

But the thing that really grabbed Garrett's attention, stood in front of the house looking like a giant insect from the realms of fantasy. With its long tail and two pairs of gossamer wings above, it gave the impression of movement even though it was standing still.

It was an old Allouette III helicopter, circa nineteen sixty.

'The old white man who might help you lives here,' said Mandla. 'We call him Old Man. He has a helicopter. And it works. He hates the Chinamen.'

'Why?' asked Garrett.

'Because he hates everybody,' answered Mandla. 'He used to be a combat pilot in the old days. Rhodesian fire force so he hates Mugabe. He hates the Chinese because he says that they are raping the country. He likes us because we also hate Mugabe. If you pay him, he will probably help you to find the Chinaman and his train.' The rebel motioned to his men. 'Stay here. You two come with me,' he said to Garrett and Petrus. 'Leave your weapons with my men.'

Doc took the two friend's rifles and then Mandla, Garrett and Petrus walked slowly towards the farmhouse door. When they were about fifty yards away a rifle shot rang out and a puff of dust leapt up next to Garrett's foot.

'Hey, Old Man, it's me, Mandla. Careful with that rifle. You might hit me with a warning shot by mistake.'

'That wasn't a warning shot,' shouted Old Man.' I was trying to hit you. Eyes aren't what they used to be.'

'Well don't, shoot again. You know me,' urged Mandla.

'True,' replied Old Man. 'But who the hell are those other two? Don't know them. What's a white man doing out here? Thought that I was the only white man for a hundred miles. Not a missionary, is he? Hate missionaries.'

'No, not missionaries,' shouted Mandla. 'They're friends of mine. They killed some Chinamen and then they helped us to kill some Fifth Brigade troops.'

'Oh well, that's okay then,' said Old man. 'Hate those fuckers even more than missionaries. Come on in.'

Another shot cracked out and whipped over their heads. All three hit the floor.

'Sorry,' shouted Old Man. 'My mistake. Slipped.'

CHAPTER THIRTY-FIVE

The inside of Old Man's house was surprisingly neat. Ancient, well-polished furniture, a dining table, a hand-woven grass mat.

Scores of original paintings covered the walls. Watercolors in vibrant color. Reds and yellow predominated. Mainly landscapes but done with a philosopher's eye, almost surreal, capturing the spirit of the land as opposed to merely recording what it looked like at the time.

Old Man himself was painfully thin. A proud six foot three shrunken by time to a bent five foot eleven. A long gray beard and mustache, hair flowed down his back, tied into a loose ponytail. Both mustache and beard were yellowed with nicotine stains. His twinkling blue eyes peered out of a weather-ravaged face with more than a hint of barely controlled insanity.

Knobbly knees stuck out below too large khaki shorts and his boots, polished to a mirror shine, looked as big as clown shoes on the end of his long spindly legs.

Garrett stared at the paintings. 'Nice,' he said.

'They're mine. I did them,' said Old Man.

'Well, they are very, very good,' commented Garrett with sincere praise.

'Yes,' agreed Old Man. 'They are.'

Garrett smiled and held out his hand. 'Pleased to meet you, sir,' he greeted. 'My name is Garrett and this here is my friend Petrus.'

Petrus nodded his hello.

Old Man shook Garrett's hand. 'Hello, young fellow. My name is...' he thought for a while, head cocked to one side. Finally, he committed himself. 'Fucked if I can remember. These bastards call me Old Man. Have done for so long I'm not even sure if I ever had another name, so I guess Old Man will have to do.' Once again, he paused in thought. 'I suppose if you want to be formal it would have to be mister Old Man, or maybe mister Man,' he rambled as he walked through to the kitchen.

'Come on,' he continued. 'Follow me. So, any of you fellows want tea or coffee?'

'Coffee would be good,' said Garrett.

Petrus nodded. 'Coffee sounds great,' he agreed.

Old Man glanced around the kitchen with an expression of confusion. Finally, he went to a cupboard and pulled out a bottle of clear liquid and four thick tumblers. 'And just where the fuck did you gentlemen think that I could get coffee?' he asked. 'The local grocers? Don't be stupid. Got this though,' he shook the bottle and then poured four tumblers full. 'Make it myself from distilled vegetable peelings.'

They all took their drinks and shot them down in one. Garrett grimaced. It tasted like benzene, raw, oily and powerful. By the time he had blinked the tears from his eyes Old Man had refilled all of their glasses.

'Now, young gentlemen,' said Old Man. 'To what do I owe the pleasure of this visit?'

So, Petrus told him their story.

Old Man nodded every now and then. He asked a few questions and he kept their glasses constantly filled, encouraging them to drink every now and then.

When Petrus' story had finished Old Man nodded. 'Right,' he said. 'Any money?'

Petrus pulled out a wad of dollars. Old Man took it from him, counted out two thousand and handed the rest back. 'That should cover expenses,' he said.

'When can we go?' asked Garrett.

'No time like the present,' replied Old Man. 'Let's fuel up and get flying.' He stood up and headed for the door, staggering slightly from the effects of the moon-shine that he had just imbibed.

They filed out of the front door and walked towards the helicopter. Mandla beckoned to his troops to join him and they all approached, chatting and laughing as they did so.

Garrett did a double take when he got close to the Allouette. The left-hand door was missing completely. There were holes in the floor and sundry wires hung from the roof, dangling down into the cockpit like lima-creepers or tentacles of some hybrid half-tree-half-machine.

'I'll get her going while you load up,' said Old Man as he clambered inside and started to flick switches and join wires together, like he was hot-wiring the machine as opposed to being its rightful owner.

Doc brought their rifles and packs over and the two friends tossed them into the back of the cab.

'I could have wished for a better ride,' said Petrus. 'This one doesn't exactly fill me with confidence. And as for the pilot…well, the less said.'

'If wishes were horses beggars would ride,' quipped Garrett.

'Yeah, and eat horse meat,' added the Zulu. 'But be that as it may, do you reckon that this heap of shit will even get airborne, let alone fly anywhere?'

'I heard that,' said Old Man. 'Now apologize or I won't take you anywhere.'

'Sorry, Old Man,' said Petrus.

'Not to me, you idiot,' said Old Man. 'You didn't insult me. Apologize to the helicopter.'

'Okay. What's its name?' asked Petrus.

'Don't be stupid,' answered Old Man. It's an inanimate object. It doesn't have a blasted name.'

'Sorry, helicopter,' said Petrus as he rolled his eyes at Garrett.

'Apology accepted,' said Old Man as he flicked a final switch.

The rotors started to spin. Very slowly, like a windmill in the mildest of zephyrs. And then they sped up. The engine coughed and spluttered and then backfired with a series of staccato shots. Smoke billowed and the rotors rotated faster and faster until they were a blur of light and steel.

Old Man unfolded a map and traced a route.

'We'll head here,' he shouted over the cacophony of the beating engine. 'It's the train line from Bulawayo to Lusaka. You say that your Chinese fellow hired himself a private train, two coaches and an engine, so he should be piss easy to spot. Most of the trains that plow that route are long bastards. Forty plus carriages. So the moment that we see a short-assed one, that's our man. I drop you off; you kill the fuckers, back in time for tea.'

'Sounds like a plan,' agreed Garrett.

Old Man nodded, flicked a final couple of switches, settled back in his seat and pushed the stick forward whilst adjusting the rudders. The helicopter screamed and bucked and shuddered into the air like an ancient swan attempting to escape the clutches of the water.

And once they were airborne the progress wasn't much better as Old Man had to constantly apply left and right rudder. It was less flying and more rodeo-bull-riding as he wrestled the helicopter into a relatively straight and level flight path.

The Allouette III travels in excess of one hundred and thirty miles an hour. However, the relic that was propelling them through the air was showing every one of its fifty years of age. The average combat helicopter has a lifespan in the region of one thousand five hundred hours before it needs a massive overhaul. Old Man's machine had probably done way over four thousand hours since its last service and overhaul. This basically meant that the tree passengers were literally flying on a wing and a prayer. Every second on the air was a second on borrowed time.

The Allouette thundered and hammered through the African sky, heading north north west as Old Man headed towards Bulawayo to pick up the tracks from there to Livingstone and the Victoria Falls.

Within two hours they had overflown the town of Bulawayo and were following the railway tracks towards the border. On their left stretched the vast plains of the Hwange National Park, the largest game park in Zimbabwe.

Old Man pointed down. 'See there,' he shouted over the cacophony of the engine and gearbox. 'That waterhole. Last year, fucking poachers dumped a barrel of Cyanide into the water. Did it to poison the elephants that drink there every night. Killed over one hundred and fifty of them. Dead elephants as far as you could see. Fucking tragic. Bastards. I helped to track the poachers down. Caught three of them. Nothing happened to them. Rumor says that some government minister was involved so the investigation was over before it even began.'

They spotted a train in the distance but as they got closer, they could see it was standard length. Over thirty coaches. Not colonel Chang's private couple.

'Getting low on fuel,' shouted The Old Man. 'Maybe twenty-five minutes. Maybe less. Hard to tell. The fuel gauge doesn't actually work.'

Ahead of them the Victoria Falls hove into view.

Again, Old Man pointed. 'Victoria Falls,' he shouted. 'Locals call it Tokoyela Tonga or The Smoke That Thunders. Over twice the height and width of Niagara Falls. Biggest waterfall in the world. We'll overfly Livingstone and keep on the track. I'll be honest with you gentlemen. What we are about to do is highly illegal. We will be entering foreign airspace with no permission. The Zambian air force has a few Mig-21's stationed at Mumbwa and Lusaka. They're pretty slack so their scramble time is closer to the hour mark as opposed to minuets. Still, they will scramble and they will come for us. General Tungata is sticky about his airspace. And I don't need to tell you, even with those useless bastards flying, they will take us down. No ifs or buts about it.'

'So, what do you recommend?' asked Garrett.

'We continue as before,' answered Old Man. 'Just warning you boys that we have time constraints. I was hoping that we could catch him while we were still in Zimbabwe, but no such luck.'

Petrus leant forward and grasped Old Man's shoulder. 'Thank you,' he said.

Old Man nodded and said nothing; instead, he concentrated on keeping his flying scrap heap airborne.

Twenty minutes later they saw the train in the distance. Two coaches being pulled by a green diesel engine. As Old Man brought them closer, they could see that there was a guard sitting on the top of each carriage.

'We need to get well ahead of them,' shouted Garrett. Then we can lay some C4 and blow the tracks.'

'Right,' answered Old Man as he adjusted the rudders and pushed the stick forward, nursing the ancient machine into a juddering increase in speed. But as they started to edge forward both of the soldiers on top of the carriages opened fire.

The sound of the high-speed rounds sticking the bodywork of the helicopters rang out loud. An insane blacksmith beating on them with a giant's hammer.

Old Man jerked the stick to the side and the helicopter shuddered sideways, the engine coughing and gasping as the revs climbed.

Garrett swung his rifle to bear on the guards and returned fire, burning off an entire magazine in one uninterrupted pull. Petrus followed suite and spent cartridges spewed into the cabin, bouncing off the windscreen and falling to the floor like falling insects.

'Something's been hit,' said Old Man. 'Oil pressure's dropping. I can't get any more speed out of her without tearing the gearbox apart.'

'Can you get us over the engine?' asked Garrett.

'Probably,' answered Old Man. 'What's the plan?'

'I'll light some short fuses on a couple of blocks of C4 and drop it on them. Blow them off the tracks.'

'We'd better be quick about this,' urged Old Man. 'Not sure how long I can keep her in the air. Also, the Migs will be scrambled soon, and we really don't want to go up against those boys.'

The helicopter pulled away from the train, keeping low and yawing from side to side in order to present a more difficult target to the gunmen on the coaches.

Garrett worked feverishly, digging through his kit to find a length of fuse, cutting it, inserting a detonator and connecting the fuse to it. Then he clapped Old Man on the shoulder.

'Let's do it.'

The helicopter thundered towards the engine that was dragging the colonel's coaches. As they approached the train Petrus leaned out of the doorway and laid down covering fire. But it was difficult to do so in an accurate manner and the helicopter juddered and swung. The soldiers on the carriage roofs had a much more stable platform to fire from and, once again, shots rang against the helicopter's body. Two rounds struck the windscreen, punching through and leaving two, star shaped holes. The instrument panel exploded in a shower of glass shards. Old Man kept the helicopter on track, flinching slightly but keeping things relatively steady.

'Almost there,' shouted Garrett as he took out his windproof Zippo and readied it.

More slugs penetrated the helicopter, buzzing and ricocheting around the cockpit like a swarm of hornets. Garrett put flame to fuse and lobbed the lumps of C4 out of the cockpit.

The first bomb landed on the line and exploded. However, although the blast blew of one of the sleepers, the train still pushed on, jerking slightly as it traversed the buckled length of track.

But the second lump of C4 landed in the open area behind the diesel engine and when it exploded it simply tore the train from the tracks. Miraculously the engine and the coaches stayed upright, simply plowing through the surrounding bush, splintering the small thorn trees in its path and eventually grinding to a stop against a small mountain of soil that it had compacted up in front of itself. As the train ground to an abrupt halt, both of the guards on the roof were thrown forward by over twenty feet and came crashing to the ground.

Old Man swept the helicopter around to the side of the derailed train and landed it with a thump.

'Right, boys,' he grunted. 'Go and get them.'

Garrett and Petrus piled out of the Allouette, rifles at port, arms pumping as they sprinted towards the train. They paid no attention to the downed guards that had been thrown from the roof, as it was obvious that they were no longer in the fight, their prostrate bodies bent and broken on the earth like discarded puppets.

Someone opened fire from the front coach and bullets whipped past the two charging friends, picking and clawing at them as they ran.

Garrett fired back, flipping his selector to full auto and dragging the rifle across the windows on the leading coach, hosing them down with a steam of superheated lead. The glass sparkled and glittered in the bright sunlight as it shattered inwards like a rain of ice.

They reached the door of the front carriage and Petrus unleashed a burst at the frame, punching the door off its hinges and into the coach. Garrett changed his magazine for a full one and ran into the carriage. Lead plucked at his clothes and a round burned across his hip. He returned fire, catching one of the Flying Tigers in the face and neck with two rounds.

There was no one else in the cabin and he ran towards the back, kicking open the adjoining door and firing as soon as he entered. The soldier in front of him fell to the floor, his chest a mire of blood and bone chips. Garrett swiveled and fired again. Another man went down, struck one of the chairs and sat down in it, leaning forward and clutching at his stomach.

Both Garrett and Petrus scouted out the rest of the carriage. It appeared to be empty.

Garrett grabbed the man sitting in the chair, pulling him upright and glancing at his rank badge on his shoulder.

'Sergeant,' he said to Petrus. 'Shit. Where is the colonel?'

Petrus raised a hand, gesturing for quiet. Both he and Garrett listened and they could hear a low whimpering coming from the back of the coach.

Garrett walked over and looked around. Finally, he saw two boots sticking out from under the last row of seats. He lent down, grabbed one and pulled. The colonel slid out.

Garrett kicked him in the ribs. 'Get up and stop sniveling.'

The colonel raised himself up to his knees and slowly stood upright. His face was a mask of abject terror and his hands were shaking.

'Please,' he said. 'Don't hurt me.'

'That depends,' said Petrus. 'Tell us, who do you work for?'

'No one,' said Chang. 'I am a free agent. Officially I suppose that I work for the Chinese government but that's all.'

Petrus shook his head. 'Wrong answer,' he said. And he shot Chang in his right knee.

The colonel fell to the floor and squirmed as he shrieked in agony. 'No. Please. Why did you do that?'

'The truth,' shouted Petrus, or I shoot the other knee.'

'His name is Tai Zeng,' said Chang through gritted teeth. 'He lives in Hong Kong. He is a Red Pole in the 14K Triad. Who are you? What do you want with me? What do you want with Tai Zeng?'

'Who am I?' asked Petrus. 'I am vengeance.'

He ejected his empty magazine and inserted a full one.

'I am retribution.'

He placed the barrel of his assault rifle against colonel Jin Chang's forehead.

'I am death.'

He pulled the trigger.

Garrett clasped his friend's shoulder. 'Come on. It is done. Time to go.'

They started to walk from the coach.

As they passed sergeant Feng, he called out to them.

'Help me,' he said. 'Have mercy.'

Garrett faced the wounded soldier.

'I am suffering,' said the sergeant. 'Please, make it quick.'

Garrett nodded. He lifted his rifle.

And Feng thought of the Huangshan Mountains. How they appeared to be almost purple in the morning sun. And the vibrant green of the rice shoots in the paddies. The lustrous velvet blackness of his sister, Mengzu's long black hair. The smell of evening jasmine.

He smiled.

And died.

Petrus jumped from the coach, followed by Garrett. They walked back towards the helicopter. It stood still, its rotors no longer moving as it squatted on the ground like a resting dragonfly.

Garrett clambered into the cockpit to update Old Man on the situation and Petrus climbed in after him. They found him slumped over the controls, his eyes closed, his arms dangling by his side. With gentle hands Garrett pulled him upright exposing a large wound in his chest.

Old Man opened his eyes and smiled. 'Fucking Chinese got me. Useless bastards, still – at least I went in the saddle, not in bed like some old infirm vegetable surrounded by nurses and machines.' He coughed and blood bubbled from his wound. 'Well,' he continued. 'Looks like you two will be walking home.'

Garrett took his hand. 'I'm sorry, Old Man,' he said, his voice barely above a whisper.

Old Man chuckled. 'Bartholomew Bridlington-Smythe,' he said.

'What?' asked Petrus.

'My name,' answered Old Man, still chuckling. 'Bartholomew Bridlington-Smythe. No wonder I forgot it. What a fucking mouthful.

He laughed again, and then died, the smile still firmly on his face.

Garrett closed Old Man's eyes and then he and Petrus took their packs and stepped out of the helicopter.

Garrett cut a strip of fabric from one of the seats. Then he opened the petrol tank, stuffed the material in and lit it. As the two of them stepped back the avgas started to burn. There wasn't much left but it was sufficient to burn long and bright, providing Old Man with a fitting funeral pyre.

Then the two of them headed north east, following the tracks. They had no desire to go back to Zimbabwe where they were still wanted fugitives.

As they walked past the derailed train Garrett took his last grenade, pulled the pin and tossed it into the carriage where the colonel and sergeant Feng had died. It exploded with a muted thud and, by the time that the two friends had walked fifty paces, the train was burning with a smoky, sullen flame.

And with it, unbeknown to them, burned the eight-thousand-dollar Hermes suitcase and its twenty-two-million-dollar contents.

CHAPTER THIRTY-SIX

It had been three weeks since Tai Zeng's empire had started to crumble. His Rhino horn supply had been utterly destroyed having had both its arms and head cut off in the form of the Russian and colonel Chang.

He had desperately attempted to replace both sections but with little to no success. Firstly, he had not even been allowed a visa to enter Zimbabwe and when he had approached the Chinese embassy in Zimbabwe they had refused to help. He had personally spoken to the ambassador Lin Chun who had literally laughed at him.

Had that happened in public, the loss of face would have been intolerable. As it was, being a private discussion, it was merely embarrassing. He had threatened the ambassador, bringing the triads into the discussion. The ambassador had retaliated by telling Tai that he would take a troop of Flying Tiger special force soldiers and he would crush the triads like a thousand-year-old egg in the hand of a titan. This had added to Tai's humiliation to such an extent that he had felt physically ill.

And now he stood, staring out at the view of Hong Kong, a full glass of whisky in his hand. The sun had set, Mingyu had gone home and he was now alone with only the bitterness of his failing empire around him.

The worst part of the whole thing was that he had no real idea what had happened. His Russian and his crew had been exterminated by a crew of men that was rumored to be as large as forty and as few as two. And then colonel Chang's Flying Tigers were decimated by the self-same people. This time, once again, the rumors that he could pick up mentioned only two men. After that, Grace Mugabe had ordered a detachment of her Fifth Brigade murderers to take out the alleged couple. They had disappeared never to be heard of again.

And Tai had no idea why any of it had happened.

Then the couple had managed to somehow find a helicopter in the middle of nowhere, track down colonel Chang, kill him and his sergeant and then simply vanish into thin air.

'Who are you?' he shouted and he threw the glass against the wall. It shattered in a storm of glass and whisky and the room filled with the pungent smell of the golden liquor.

'We are the shepherds of Malusi's soul,' said a voice behind him.

He spun around. Standing in the shadows, in the corner of his office, stood a man. Six foot plus, perhaps two hundred and twenty pounds of muscle and bone. His black hair tumbled to his shoulders in glossy curls.

His jaw was unshaven, rough with a couple of day's growth.

His eyes were the deepest green, jade pools of emerald fire. Tai Zeng knew that, for the first time in his life, he was staring directly into the abyss.

And then the man threw his head back and howled like a beast. Tai swore that he saw the man's eyes change color, glowing like red coals in the darkness and he felt a tremor of absolute terror thrill through his body as, for a moment, his very bowels turned to liquid.

But the triad enforcer was made of tough stuff and he recovered quickly, stepping forward and striking out with the Ving Tsun method of rolling punches. Nothing landed and when he cast his head around, he saw that the man beast had already moved across the room. Tai blinked and drove forward once again, throwing more punches as soon as he was within range.

This time the man did not move away. Instead, he simply brushed Tai's blows aside, like a lion fighting a monkey. Zeng spun on his back foot, bringing his leading leg up, ready to strike a viscous roundhouse kick. Before his foot could land, he felt a crushing blow to his larynx and the world started to go black.

He staggered back, lurching and choking until he banged up against his desk. With a supreme effort he stood upright and faced the man beast once more.

But when he tried to focus on him it was almost impossible to differentiate between him and the shadow that seemed to surround him.

He was like a wraith. A yaomo or demon. The eater of souls.

Then the shadow came alive once again and struck him in the center of his chest.

The pain was indescribable. Tai fell back onto his desk, his arms thrown wide as he drowned in a sea of agony and terror.

And the last thing that he saw before he died were the two green eyes of the yaomo.

CHAPTER THIRTY-SEVEN

As always, Mingyu arrived early.

To arrive late was to invite a lesson in obedience from mister Zeng.

And Tai Zeng was not a man that you would want to be disciplined by.

She boiled the kettle and prepared a cup of chai for mister Zeng, placing it on his small ivory tray and taking it through to his office. She hoped that he would not demand any favors of her as she was still raw and painful from the morning before.

When she saw his body, she dropped the tray.

Then she smiled.

He lay across his desk, arms spread like a crucifix, his face a rictus of pure agony.

And in his chest, rammed through to his very spine, was a dark, polished rhino horn.

CHAPTER THIRTY-EIGHT

Petrus stood and looked down at Malusi's grave. The sun had just risen and the African dawn chorus was tuning up. The soft cooing of gray doves, the deep lowing of the royal cows, the melodious singing of the young women as they walked down to the river to collect water.

'It is done, my brother,' he said, his voice thick with emotion. 'It is done.'

Above him an African Eagle called. Its cry a strident command, cutting through the morning chorus.

Petrus watched the raptor climb higher and higher into the red sky, until he could no longer see it anymore.

And the Zulu prince smiled.

'Yes,' he said. 'It is over. Goodbye my brother.'

****

Well, that's it once more. I sincerely hope that you enjoyed this latest adventure. Garrett and Petrus will be back soon in - "Savage Outcome".

If you would like to discuss anything, please feel free to email at *zuffs@sky.com*.

Thanks again - Craig

Once again - this was for Polly and Axel - they all are.

Here's a sample of the next Garrett & Petrus book…

SAVAGE OUTCOME

Flight SA107 touched down on the tarmac at Edinburgh airport at five fifteen AM.

The tall, muscular Zulu was amongst the first passengers to alight, leaving the business class cabin with no hand luggage and walking purposefully across the link and into the terminal building. He glanced out of the small windows and grimaced at the weather. It was still as dark as midnight and the driving sleet eddied and scurried around the yellow sodium spotlights like clouds of moths around a candle flame.

The people outside were bundled up in layers of clothing, heavy boots, jackets, scarves and gloves. The Zulu owned no gloves. Nor a scarf. He had never had a need for such clothing.

He wore faded jeans, hiking boots and a heavy plaid blanket shirt that he had purchased in deference to the sub-zero temperatures.

A bored passport officer flicked through the proffered green passport, checked his entry visa and stamped it. He looked as if he were about to fall asleep. No questions were asked. Not even the standard, 'business or pleasure'. The Zulu nodded his thanks and continued on to the luggage retrieval area.

He picked up his luggage at the carousel, a battered olive-green military issue rucksack. The fasteners had been padlocked with cheap but heavy cast iron locks and the carry straps had been replaced at some stage with two, wide hand-tooled leather straps. Various rents and tears in the canvas had been roughly stitched with thick Dacron twine. Patches had been cobbled over a row of punctures that looked suspiciously like bullet holes. Frankensteinian surgery. A resurrection of something that should have been long dead.

The backpack was almost as scarred as its owner.

He walked unchecked through the customs area, following the 'nothing-to-declare' route and past the arrival gates into the main terminal, scanning the waiting crowd as he did so.

The man that he was looking for stood out easily. Slightly over six feet tall, long black hair that curled down to his shoulders. Three or four day's growth of beard. Deep set eyes, as green as a lover's grave. A long length brown leather Barbour coat. Military issue boots. Jeans. Broad shoulders tapering down to narrow hips.

Although the terminal was thronging with people, there was a small area of calm about the man with the green eyes. As if a force shield kept all at least two or three feet away from him. A shark surrounded by sardines.

The Zulu walked up to the man with the green eyes.

'Garrett,' he said.

'Petrus,' responded the man.

They both burst out laughing and hugged each other roughly, banging each other on the back.

Garrett led the way to the car park and the two of them chatted away like a pair of schoolboys after a summer break. When they reached the Land Rover, Petrus threw his old rucksack onto the back seat and then they pulled off, stopping at the exit to pay.

Garrett drove down Glasgow Road heading for the M90, lights on and average speed down in the crowded traffic.

The heater blasted out hot air, fighting the frigid winter morning, warming the cab to an acceptable temperature. But when they hit the highway Petrus opened his window, allowing a tide of arctic air into the cab, dropping the temperature to below freezing in an instant.

'Hey,' complained Garrett.

Petrus took a deep breath. 'Sorry,' he said. 'I had to smell the land. I've been locked inside a tin can for a whole night and then straight into the car. I feel like I've been buried alive.' He dragged more of the cold air into his lungs and then sighed. 'That's better,' he said as he wound the window up and settled back into his seat again.

They drove on for another half an hour and then a gas station hove into view on the side of the freeway. Garrett glanced at his gas tank and decided to pull in and fill up.

The two of them went into the kiosk to pay and, at the same time Garrett purchased two black coffees. Petrus went to the self serve counter and ladled six spoons of sugar into his cup before he took a sip.

'Gas is expensive here,' he noted as he watched Garrett hand over a wad of notes.

'More than double South Africa, but I suppose it's all relative,' said Garrett.

'Relative to what?'

Garrett shrugged. 'Actually, I don't know,' he admitted. 'But isn't that what everyone says?'

Petrus laughed and followed his friend back to the car. He glanced at his watch. 'Nine o'clock and the sun is just coming up.'

'Yep,' agreed Garrett. 'Enjoy it while you can. It goes down at half past three.'

'Will it get any warmer?'

Garrett shook his head. 'Colder, actually.'

Petrus sighed. 'Oh well,' he said. 'At least no one is shooting at us.'

They both burst out laughing.

The trip took a little under four hours and, by the time they cruised into the main gates of the laird's estate the sun was already low in the sky, squinting embarrassedly through the thick cloud cover.

Garrett turned off the sweeping driveway before he got to the main house and took a smaller narrow track for almost half a mile, eventually pulling up outside a thatched stone cottage.

'My house,' said Garrett.

Petrus grabbed his rucksack and followed Garrett into the cottage. It was a small, single room abode. A rudimentary kitchen area ran down the one wall, wood burning stove, a butler sink, running water a small refrigerator and a few cupboards.

On the opposite wall a large fireplace that had already been laid. Four small shuttered windows, a single bed, opposite was a new camp bed for Petrus.

Two old leather armchairs were situated on each side of a low teak coffee table. An outside bookcase on the one wall, packed with books as diverse as Shakespeare, beat author Jack Kerouac and the Garfield's Fat Cat three pack by Jim Davis. Petrus found Shakespeare to be obtuse and Kerouac pretentious. He liked the cat.

The Zulu approved. It was a man's dwelling, no fripperies or false finery. He threw his rucksack onto the camp bed and then started to undo the straps while Garrett put flame to the fire.

Petrus opened his pack and pulled out a few items. 'Here,' he said to Garrett. 'I brought you some cigars at duty free. Cuban.' He handed over a box of twenty five Esplendidos.

Garrett grinned. 'Thanks,' he said. 'These are great.'

'Also, I brought this,' said Petrus. 'You forgot it when you last left.' He pulled out a large machete. It was sheathed in a shoulder holster that had been converted to accommodate the long blade. 'I also brought my assegai,' continued Petrus as he drew his lethal short spear from his pack. The eighteen inch blade and short handle just fitted in the rucksack, packed in from corner to corner.

'Jesus,' said Garrett. 'How did you get this stuff through customs?'

Petrus shrugged. 'No one asked if I was carrying a spear and a machete, so I didn't tell them.'

'Well you were lucky.'

'Got anything to drink?' asked Petrus.

'Loads, but I thought that we could go and meet the laird first.'

Petrus pulled a face. 'Tomorrow,' he said. 'Tonight we smoke cigars, sit by the fire, drink brandy and talk. Tomorrow we do the whole meet and greet thing.'

Garrett smiled and nodded. 'Right. Tomorrow.'

And so they settled in beside the fire and talked deep into the night. Drinking cognac, smoking the Esplendidos and discussing past and future happenings.

Communicating in half sentences and in jokes, as only close friends could. Teasing and insulting and complimenting in equal measures.

Eventually the fire burned low and they both crawled into their respective beds and found sleep.

Garrett touched Petrus on the shoulder and the Zulu came instantly awake, his right hand reaching for his assegai.

'It's me,' said Garrett. 'Time to rise and shine.' He thrust a mug of black coffee into Petrus' hands.

The Zulu took a noisy sip. 'What time is it?'

'Seven o'clock.'

'It's still pitch black outside,' observed Petrus.

'Until almost ten o'clock,' said Garrett.

'What's for breakfast?'

'We'll be eating with the laird,' answered Garrett. 'So I'm not sure what we'll get but there will be lots.'

After Petrus had risen and performed the three S's, shit, shower and shave, the two of them climbed into the Land Rover and drove to the main house. As they approached, the huge gray stone edifice loomed out of the slowly gathering light. A building as stolid and ugly as it was imposing. A massive brooding testament to Edwardian era wealth.

Garrett pulled up to the back of the house and they entered via a side entrance.

'Servants entrance,' quipped Petrus.

Garrett shook his head. 'No, the family use this entrance. The front door is simply too huge and it's far away from all the rooms that they use to live in. Kitchen, drawing rooms and so on. The front of the house is all entrance hall and ballroom and formal dining area.'

Petrus followed Garrett through a maze of corridors and into a large dining area. A twenty seat table dominated the center of the room. High ceilings, large arched windows, deep pile maroon carpets and wood paneled walls. Along the one wall stood a heavy sideboard, on it an array of silver food cloches covered a variety of serving platters. Alongside them stood dewed glass jugs of freshly squeezed fruit juices as well as two tea pots and a Bunn flask of coffee.

Next to the buffet stood a man. A similar height to Garrett, gray messy collar length hair, an unlit pipe clenched between his teeth. He wore a kilt, white shirt and tweed jacket. Booted feet. Long faced with large ears and a prominent nose. He looked up at the two friends as they approached and his face lit up with a smile.

Garrett turned to Petrus and said. 'Petrus, may I introduce The Much Honored, Brody Macaslan, Laird of Braegorm.'

Petrus bowed deeply. 'I greet you, *Inkosi*,' he said, using the traditional Zulu word for Lord or Chief.

'Braegorm,' continued Garrett, addressing the laird correctly by his territorial designation, as opposed to his name. 'May I introduce to you, *inkosana* Dinangwe, known also as Petrus Sizwe Dlamini, eldest son of chief Dlamini of Drummond, the Valley of a Thousand Hills.'

The laird bowed back. 'Splendid,' he said as he shook Petrus' hand, struggling momentarily as the Zulu shook in the African way, reversing his grip halfway through and then changing back. 'Well now that's over with,' continued the laird. 'Please call me Brody,'

The Zulu smiled. 'Please call me Petrus,' he countered.

'Good,' said Brody as he clapped his hands together. 'Now, let's eat. The rest of the guests tend to sleep in so we may as well start without them, heaven knows when the blighters will actually deign to turn up.'

Petrus needed no encouragement as he grabbed a plate and started to lift the silver cloches and help himself to a variety of breakfast foods. Then, one hand holding a plate piled high with sausage, devilled kidney, bacon, gammon, fried eggs and black pudding, and the other carrying a mug of black coffee, he set himself down at the table.

Garrett followed with a more modest plateful of kedgeree and black pudding and a mug of black coffee.

The laird fixed himself a bowl of oat porridge with heaps of sugar and a large dash of Laphroaig whisky as opposed to milk.

As they started to eat a women entered the room. Small and pale, blonde hair cropped short, eyes outlined in thick coal, pink lips shiny with transparent gloss. She wore brown moleskin trousers, a cream linen blouse and ankle boots.

All three men stood up.

'My dear,' greeted the laird.

She nodded and then looked at Petrus.

The laird gestured towards the Zulu. 'This is Prince Petrus Dlamini,' he said. 'Petrus, this is my granddaughter, Alicia.'

'I've heard of you,' she said, her voice surprisingly low and breathy. Like a forty a day smoker.

'Good things, I hope,' grinned Petrus.

She shook her head. 'No.'

Petrus raised an eyebrow but said nothing in return, instead he simply sat down and continued attacking his mountain of fried protein.

Alicia helped herself to a cup of tea. Milk no sugar. She sat down at the far end of the table and stared out of the window while the men finished their food, then she lit a cigarette.

'Alicia, darling,' said the laird. 'Not at the breakfast table, please.'

Alicia stared at the laird for a while as she took another two puffs. And then she dropped the glowing butt into her tea. The laird winced as the water fizzed and a small swirl of smoke rose from the cup. Then he turned to Garrett.

'My boy,' he said. 'There will be four of us for the shoot. Myself, Sir Rupert, Colonel Ruttington and Wilfred Willbourne. They've all got their own rifles so no problems there.'

Garrett nodded. 'They do know that they will only be allowed to bag does, don't they?' asked Garrett. 'Shooting season for trophy bucks is finished.'

'Told them,' affirmed the laird. 'The fellows simply want to get out in the open and take a few pot shots. Tell you what, let's go to the gun room and select a couple of rifles for you and Petrus. We can discuss the shoot on the way.'

'Garrett glanced at Petrus. 'You coming?' he asked.

'I'll take care of the prince,' said Alicia. 'Give him a tour of the old place, get him acclimatized.'

'Splendid,' exclaimed the laird as he left the room followed closely by Garrett.

Alicia lit another cigarette and stared at Petrus. The Zulu returned her gaze, calmly and without rancor, and finally she dropped her eyes and stood up.

'Come on,' she said. 'Follow me; I'll give you the full guided tour.'

Petrus followed her as she left the dining room, casually flicking her ash onto the floor as she went.

'That's the breakfast, or small dining room,' she said as they exited. 'The formal dining room is at the front of the house.' They meandered down a vast corridor and she pointed out rooms as they walked past. 'The top two floors are pretty much all bedrooms. I think about forty-six or so. Library, drawing room, study, second kitchen.'

The list seemed endless and as Petrus walked about the mansion, he noticed that, although some rooms were staggering in their display of opulence, others were literally falling apart with loose plaster on the walls and holes in the ceilings. An eclectic mix of prince and pauper.

'We have over four thousand acres of land with a loch, and twenty-two miles of river frontage,' continued Alicia as she lit another cigarette from the smoldering butt of her last one. 'But I suppose that you're used to all this sort of shit,' she said. 'What is your dad, some sort of African king?'

Petrus shook his head. 'No. The king of the Zulus is King Goodwill Zwelithini kaBhekuzulu. My father is an *Inkosi*. A chief of the tribe.'

'But you are a prince?'

'Loosely speaking,' agreed Petrus. 'I am an *inkosana*. That translates to prince but it also means simply the eldest son of an *Inkosi*.'

'So do you live in a palace?'

Petrus smiled. 'My father has the second biggest house in the village. My mother, his first wife, has the biggest. My hut is no bigger than Garrett's cottage. Smaller actually.'

'But we have over sixty rooms here,' stated Alicia. She sounded disappointed.

'I can see that,' admitted Petrus. 'But you see, in Africa we have no need for such a multitude of rooms, many that simply sit and rot. We have not yet found a need for such rooms.' Petrus was vaguely amused by the massive stately home but he managed to keep his grin to a minimum.

Alicia glowered at the Zulu.

'I'm going back to my rooms,' she said to Petrus. 'I'm sure that you can show yourself out.'

Petrus nodded his goodbye as he watched her leave.

As she turned the corner at the end of the corridor, she heard his deep chuckle reverberate through the hallway and she walked faster to escape the sound.

CHAPTER THREE

Sir Rupert carried a Westley Richards .375 H&H rifle. He stood six feet five inches tall and probably weighed as much as a medium size fourteen-year-old boy. Garrett had met him before and found him to be a genuinely nice person, albeit a clichéd caricature of the quintessential English upper-class twit. No chin, large nose and ears and bad teeth.

The colonel had a Banser .300 WSM, a good all-purpose rifle that was well kept and well used. However, one look at the colonel's eye glasses and it was obvious that shooting with him would most probably involve more luck than skill. Garrett had never seen such thick lenses before. They were the proverbial bottom-of-a-coke-bottle. And to compound his terrible sight the colonel appeared to be almost totally deaf as well, causing him to bark his sentences at top volume whenever he spoke.

Wilfred Willbourne was the third guest and he sported a hand finished Holland & Holland 30-06 rifle with a Mauser action. A hunting rifle that most likely cost more than the average family home in the United Kingdom. He was a short man who stood tall, his flabby stomach bulging over his too-tight trousers and his chest filled his shirt as taut as a sausage-skin. Jaw aggressively thrust forward, slightly knock-kneed and a doughy face with bright red cheeks. He looked at both Garrett and Petrus with distain and, when introduced, deigned to shake Garrett's proffered hand.

Petrus had declined a rifle, claiming that he couldn't be bothered to carry a weapon on his holidays.

They had used the Land Rover to get past the loch and into the interior of the estate, amongst the foothills of the surrounding mountains. An area that literally teemed with both Roe and Red deer.

When they all climbed out of the car, the colonel beckoned to Garrett.

'I say, chap, I wonder if your Askari could carry my rifle?' he bellowed, pointing at Petrus. 'Got a touch of arthritis in the shoulder and it's playing up a bit.'

Garrett's face immediately assumed a thunderous expression, but before he could say anything Petrus ran over, came to attention in front of the colonel and saluted.

'Me be honored to carry your rifle, *Bwana*,' he said with a wide grin. 'Me take top care of it, *Bwana* colonel sir.'

The colonel handed his rifle over and Petrus saluted again and slung the strap over his shoulder.

'You're not funny, you know,' whispered Garrett to his friend.

'Well, I had to do something before you lashed out at the old bugger.'

'He's a racist prick,' continued Garrett.

Petrus shook his head. 'No, he's not. He's just old and ignorant.'

Willbourne strode over to Petrus and held out his rifle. 'There you go, chap,' he said. 'Might as well carry mine as well while you're about it.'

Petrus stared at the pudgy man and then shook his head. 'In your dreams, boy.'

Willbourne glared at the Zulu but Petrus simply ignored him.

Garrett set off along a trail, checking for spoor as he did so and the rest of the men followed him with Petrus bringing up the rear.

After half an hour or so Garrett held up his hand, clenching his fist in a signal to halt. Then he beckoned to the laird who walked up next to him.

Garrett pointed across the valley. 'There,' he said in a low voice. 'A stag and three hinds. We need to work our way to the right, over by the stone cairn. Should be able to get a good shot then.'

Willbourne stomped over and peered at the small herd. 'I think that I'll take a pot shot from here,' he announced as he unslung his rifle.

Garrett shook his head. 'No. We need to get closer.'

'Bullshit,' stated Willbourne. 'If we try to get any closer, we'll scare them off. I reckon that I should take a shot.'

Petrus walked over and looked at the deer. 'It's easy to get closer,' he said.

'Rubbish,' responded Willbourne. 'Just because you live in the bush doesn't make you an authority on deer hunting, good fellow.'

Petrus raised an eyebrow but said nothing.

Garrett started to talk to the laird but his sentence was cut off as Willbourne raised his rifle to his shoulder and fired. The shot went wide and the herd scattered and ran.

'I told you not to shoot,' said Garrett through gritted teeth.

'So what,' said Willbourne. 'I don't have to listen to the hired help.'

'Really, Wilfred,' interjected the laird. 'Why don't you come off it, old chap? You really are acting like the worst sort.'

Willbourne looked suitably chastised but that didn't stop him mumbling under his breath. 'I'll take the shot when I want to, bloody hell.'

Garrett composed himself and led the party down a different track, once again casting for fresh spoor. Forty minutes later he pointed out another small herd. Two hinds and a stag.

'So you reckon that you can get closer?' sneered Willbourne at Petrus.

The Zulu stared at the podgy man for a few seconds then he simply stood up and handed the colonel's rifle to Garrett, taking off his blanket shirt as he did.

Underneath, he had on his shoulder rig, containing his assegai.

His bare torso rippled with muscle and the weak winter sun threw his countless scars into stark relief. Long ragged slash wounds, short indented stab wounds and a row of puckered holes that were obviously bullet scars.

He drew his blade with a steel rasp and Willbourne took a step back, his face drained of all color as his eyes fixated on the two feet of razor-sharp steel.

Without a word, Petrus turned and ran into the heather and the gorse, his steps long and loping. Smooth as a thoroughbred race horse. Within seconds he had simply disappeared. Vanishing into the landscape like he was part of it.

'What the fuck?' stammered Willbourne.

The colonel gave a chuckle. 'Seen this sort of thing before, don't you know,' he said. 'Maasai warriors. Saw one kill a lion with a spear once. Bloody impressive.' He walked over to Willbourne, leaning in close as he spoke. As if he was sharing an intimate secret. 'Word of advice, Wilf, old chap. I'd watch my mouth if I were you. Chances are, if you keep offending the Askari, he'll gut you like a fish. I remember the Mau Mau in Kenya, 1953, night of the long knives. I was stationed there with The Black Watch, bloody locals went on a rampage, gutted a whole bunch of unsuspecting colonials. We had to discipline them of course, ending up killing over five thousand of the buggers.

Great weather though, always sunny, don't you know?' He chuckled to himself and took out a pipe that he clenched between his teeth without lighting. 'Gut you like a fish,' he repeated.

Willbourne delved into his shooting jacket and drew out a silver flask that he uncapped and took a swig from. The smell of single malt whisky wafted through the group.

Garrett kept his eyes on the herd of deer, trying to spot Petrus as he stalked them even though he knew it to be a waste of time and effort. If his friend did not want to be seen then he simply would not be seen.

There was a flurry of movement and the small herd scattered and disappeared over the crest of the hill.

'Ha,' declared Willbourne. 'So much for that. Scared them away, just as I said.'

But Garrett said nothing because he had been watching much closer than the others, so he was the only one to notice that, out of the herd of three animals, only two ran over the hill.

'Come along then,' said Willbourne with a smirk on his face. 'Farce is over, let's continue.'

Garrett raised his hand. 'Just a moment, mister Willbourne,' he said. 'Let's wait for Petrus.'

'Why?'

'Because he's part of the group,' snapped the laird. 'That's why, Willbourne.'

Once again, the podgy man looked a little sheepish and, once again, he muttered a comeback under his breath. 'Don't see why we have to wait for him. Bloody cheeky sod that he is.'

So the men waited. The colonel chewed on the stem of his pipe. Willbourne drank from his flask, without offering, and mumbled to himself as he did so. And Garrett and the laird stood patiently and scouted the landscape.

Suddenly, and without warning Petrus appeared out of the long grass, like a wraith rising from a grave. Over his shoulders he carried a two-hundred-pound hind. Its throat had been cut and the blood had run down Petrus' shoulders and onto his chest. He dropped the carcass down at Willbourne's feet and then he raised his assegai above his head and shouted.

'*Ngadla!* I have eaten!' Then he leant towards the podgy man and said in a voice as low as a lover's whisper and as clear as thunder. 'You see, it is possible to get closer.' Willbourne shrank back. 'And the next time that you speak to me,' continued Petrus. 'You will address me as *inkosana* Dinangwe, or prince Dinangwe. Not boy, or fellow, or chap. Do you understand?'

Willbourne nodded, his movements jerky and uncoordinated as fear stole his ability to perform simple motor skills.

'Good,' said Petrus as he stole a sly sideways glance at the colonel. 'Because if you forget, I may have to gut you like a fish.'

The colonel burst out laughing.

www.ingramcontent.com/pod-product-compliance
Lightning Source LLC
Chambersburg PA
CBHW061317190726
48288CB00002B/538